THE SITTERS

Published in Penguin

The Tivington Nott
The Ancestor Game

THE SITTERS

Alex Miller

Viking

Viking
Penguin Books Australia Ltd
487 Maroondah Highway, PO Box 257
Ringwood, Victoria 3134, Australia
Penguin Books Ltd
Harmondsworth, Middlesex, England
Viking Penguin, A Division of Penguin Books USA Inc.
375 Hudson Street, New York, New York 10014 USA
Penguin Books Canada Limited
10 Alcorn Avenue, Toronto, Ontario, Canada M4V 3B2
Penguin Books (N.Z.) Ltd
182-190 Wairau Road, Auckland 10, New Zealand

First published by Penguin Books Australia, 1995
10 9 8 7 6 5 4 3 2 1
Copyright © A. & S. Miller Pty Ltd, 1995

Typeset in Australia by Midland Typesetters
Made and Printed in Australia by Australian Print Group

National Library of Australia
Cataloguing-in-Publication data:
Miller, Alex
The sitters.
ISBN 0 670 86231 2
I. Title.
A823.3

for Stephanie

I am grateful to Bryony Cosgrove for her critical support and impeccable judgement.

The trained hand often knows more than the head.

Paul Klee

When I was old and could no longer hope for new friendships, one of the saddest episodes of my life began to come back to me and to offer me my greatest joy. Under the influence of this memory, revisiting me in its new disguise, I was able to paint again. For the gift had left me. I don't believe I'll ever suffer such a paralysis of my will again. Now I'll go on painting until the end. Which must be the hope of every artist. Simply to work.

And that is what she gave me, Jessica Keal, the subject of this altered memory, a memory entangled with certain family likenesses and forgotten moments of my childhood; her roots and mine mysteriously grown together. That entire episode is contained for me in a single image. And although there's only one figure in this image – for it's my portrait of Jessica that I'm talking about – it's an image in which I'm content, for once, to recognise myself. As I remember her, I remember myself and am able to approach the last enigma of my life – my family and my childhood. That cold legacy of silence and absence.

I first saw Jessica in Canberra at a university function put on by her department to welcome her. They weren't my people at the function and I hadn't been invited to attend it, but I happened to be passing and saw that food and drink were available in the common room, and as it was almost lunchtime I went in and helped myself. She was already the centre of attention and was surrounded by a curious and animated group of women and men on the far side of the room.

In my memory of her that day Jessica has dark hair that gleams with an auburn light and falls in a soft line at the nape of her neck. There are purplish shadows of fatigue and uncertainty beneath her eyes. She's wearing a summer dress. The dress is a fine one, an expensive dress – as if it is to be her confidence on a day when other things may fail her. The dress is made of some dark material. It may even be black, but it has a motif of some kind in a silvery colour that relieves the sombreness and the stillness of the fabric. The straps of the dress press into the flesh of her shoulders. Her bare arms give an impression of strength but also of refinement, for she holds herself erect and looks about her with a detached curiosity. Of course, she's a visitor and has just arrived, which might explain this look of detachment. But it's also something that belongs to her. She's like that. Observing her you might imagine there's something Mediterranean in her ancestry, perhaps even Spanish. This, and her air of detachment, remind me of the woman who in my youth convinced me that the artist's occupation could be a noble thing, for *she* had been like that, handsome and aloof and troubled. Jessica looks directly at the person who's speaking to her but gives the impression, nevertheless, that she's not with that person. She's withholding herself. She is wary, of the company and of her situation and of herself. In her left hand she holds an unlit cigarette, which she looks at every so often but does not light. Her ambivalence and uncertainty add to her charms for me.

I stayed longer and drank more wine than I'd intended. She must have been aware of my scrutiny, and eventually she turned and looked directly at me. Her gaze was filled with enquiry and challenge, and even with a certain enmity, as if she thought that in me she'd detected the cause of her predicament and unease. Well, what is it you want from me? her look demanded, though naturally she didn't actually say this. It was no more than a fleeting moment. A strong look from across the room letting me know of her annoyance. Then she looked away.

The wine had by then had a considerable effect, and I laughed at my own discomfort. You can't feel that tremor inside you, however, that signal that something deeper than usual has been touched by another person, without believing the experience to have been shared. So although I left the common room that day without speaking to Jessica, I continued to think about her for several weeks, and whenever I was at the university I looked out for her. Then eventually I began to forget her, the way we do when nothing further happens to make vivid once more an encounter that has disturbed us and left us feeling restless and dissatisfied. An experience that has reminded us that happiness is absent from our lives. By the time I saw her again I'd more or less given up expecting to see her. I was caught off-guard and didn't manage that meeting very well either.

It was late one evening and I was going home from

the university. The end of a harrowing day for me. I was feeling old and angry, shuffling along to the lifts with an image of myself in my mind as a caved-in grey old man. Not the kind of person strangers go out of their way to talk to. Someone was coming along the corridor towards me. She stopped in front of me and I expected a question, expected her to ask directions from me.

She was wearing a jacket and jeans and she had her hair done differently. I didn't recognise her.

'Hullo,' she said.

It took me a couple of seconds to realise it was her. 'I'm sorry,' I said. 'I didn't recognise you.' I asked her how she was settling in and she said things were going well for her. I went along to the lift. I didn't hesitate, didn't hang around. I left her standing there. It was partly due to the decrepit self-image of the moment.

It wasn't until I woke in the early morning that I admitted to myself there'd been this little place of trust, this little offer, between us at our chance meeting in the corridor. And then I had the time to reflect and I realised I'd missed the sequel to the common room encounter. I'd let it go by. And an enormous feeling of regret came over me.

I lay in bed listening to the sounds before dawn and thinking about her. I elaborated what might have been the possibilities of our meeting if I hadn't scuttled away like a scared hermit. I sought out a sense of her gravity, the genuine loneliness of the person who doesn't lie to themselves about this, and it made her deeply attractive to me, the person I was imagining. Her detachment a kind of grandeur. A quality I admired more than anything. I saw her turn towards me, her bare arms, the straps of her dress pressing into her shoulders, her fingers holding the unlit cigarette. And I saw her turn away again. The withholding of herself that was the foreground of something of great substance, some unshakeable purpose, a private and unspoken intention that she had dwelt on with care and singleness of mind over the decades of her life. I played with this idea and drew it out and pursued it. And I did this at that hour of the morning when it's possible for me to believe that suicide is my most rational course for the day. I regretted my failure to acknowledge the little pool of trust between us, the offer that could never be repeated, arising from circumstances peculiar to the moment. And I watched that woman, Jessica Keal, standing there in the corridor at the university waiting for me to recognise her.

I saw there had been a feeling then that she'd wanted to put her hand on my arm, perhaps to say something to me. Something reassuring and intimate that would have given a lift to our spirits and brought us together. The remembrance of seeing her in the common room and then leaving without speaking to her. That open connection between us swirling around with my regrets. And I wondered what she'd seen this time. An old man coming along the corridor. Crumpled. Devastated by all those years of feverish work and ambition.

I didn't get up at my usual early hour and go in to the studio and begin work. Instead, I stayed in bed thinking about her till the sun was well up and shining through the blinds into my room. Her dark eyes with the soft purplish shadows beneath them and their suggestion of some deep inner trouble and their aggressive question to me still hanging in the air unanswered, *What do you want from me?* I wanted the chance to deal with all that.

I never painted the members of my family, either my old childhood family in England or my new family in Australia. I left my home when I was fifteen, and although I revisited my people many times over the years, even working in England for a time, I was never able to paint their portraits. This blindness with regard to my intimates always struck me as a severe limitation of my vision, a real handicap, and even as something that might finally cripple me and invalidate altogether my entire work as a painter of portraits. And it wasn't something that was overlooked by the critics either. I didn't like to think about it. It was too large an absence. I was never able to deal with it, this unpainted childhood. No one ever mentioned it to me without me getting angry and defensive. I could never see a way of breaking the deadlock of it. I'd lived away from my parents and my sister for most of my life, and my Australian wife and son had left Canberra years ago. I didn't know who any of these people had become. My family was represented by this remarkable silence in my work. It was something I never tackled. Most of the time I didn't think about them. Whenever something happened that required me to consider them, I'd be troubled and unhappy until I could distract myself from them again by returning to my work. My son would visit me from time to time. He'd bring his wife and two children and we'd pretend to be a family again. But I found his visits unsettling and distracting and was glad when he left again and the house was mine once more. It made me feel guilty to see my grandchildren and my beautiful daughter-in-law and my successful son.

My father taught me to draw. If it were summer when he was home on a twenty-four-hour leave during the war, he would take us on a Greenline bus out into the country. We'd get off the bus in some out-of-the-way village in Kent and we'd look for a sheltered spot in a field, under an old elm tree or close against a piece of woodland, where we would be alone and out of the sight of passers-by. And in this secluded corner my mother and sister and my father and I would establish our camp, as if we'd decided to become gypsies, and we'd settle down there with our bits and pieces until nightfall. Going home at the end of the day, rushing along the dark lanes with the overhanging branches of the trees snatching at the windows of the bus, we'd sit close, carrying the solitude of the country back with us into the housing estate and thinking our thoughts in silence together.

The way I saw it, on these occasions I was the one to carry the old walnut box he kept his paints and brushes and pencils in. Although he'd bought the box from a street stall I decided it had been in his possession forever. It smelt as he smelt, of aromatic wood and paints and sharpened pencils and tobacco, and I couldn't see that box without seeing his nicotine-stained fingers jiggling a brush in the little pot of cloudy water, and hearing his hushed voice describing to me the intricate problems of the scene before us — as if we were hunters concealed in the covert and planning our strategy, being careful not to startle our shy quarry. His grandfather had been a gamekeeper in Scotland, so maybe something of that style was bred in him; and in me too if I'm forced to concede it, the covert and the hidden, the desire to conceal myself, to steal up on things without being seen, to catch my models in the privacy of their thoughts.

And when he'd gone back to the war, transformed once again into a soldier in his khaki uniform, carrying his heavy rifle and his pack, after I'd watched him from the window of our flat until the very last second, until he'd turned the corner at the top of the street and had looked back and saluted me gravely for the last time, then I hid under the table and pressed my nose against the precious painting box and breathed its rich sad smell and I cried for a long time. I could cry for him easily then.

With our brushes and our saucers of water and colour, we'd draw our intricate scenes of coppices and fields and church spires in the distance, and we'd take care to render our clouds fluffy and light and to set them delicately in a china-blue sky. And while we painted he'd tell me his dreams, for me and for himself and for our life after the war. And that's what I'd begun to live for, these strange, beautiful and romantic fancies, this future that was never going to be part of our real lives, but which belonged to a more socially elaborate style than anything we would ever know.

The truth is – and it's not an easy matter for me to stick to the truth when I'm talking about my father – we went only once into the country on an excursion like that, and even then it was not quite like that anyway. But let's say at least that the experience of that one real imperfect day in the green field in Kent left an impression in me of perfection nevertheless. Happiness. That's what it was, summer and the closeness of my family and the possibility of dreams. A delusive little memory, kneaded and pummelled and stretched out endlessly by my longings and by my imagination, until it eventually filled a whole period of my childhood and I had transformed it into an endowment worth living for. And perhaps I made that day into such a large imaginary life so that it would reduce the space left in my real history for the brutal period that followed it, when the war was over and he was at home for good, so damaged and charged with bitterness that he never dreamed for us again.

It was always portraits with me. Portraits of other people. For forty years my work was images of strangers. Then it changed. She brought about the change. I don't know how it happened. It's a story, not an explanation.

I like plain things. I like to bring all that chaos and noise back to an image that has a certain amount of silence in it. My furniture is plain. When she saw my place Jessica said, 'You've got what you need.' She knew what she meant. Plain things have their own excellence. In sumptuous surroundings I feel lonely. In grand houses I've always felt abandoned. My house in Canberra was an ex-Government house where a middle-level public servant had lived. The previous owner had built a verandah onto the back. That was all. When my wife and son left I had the verandah closed in with big windows and I opened the wall of

the back bedroom so that the bedroom and the verandah formed a large L-shaped space. That was my
studio, the place where I worked and where I stored
my stuff. It was where I spent all my time. People
were often taken aback by this. They were disappointed when they came to see me for the first time
and saw how simply I lived. They felt cheated that
there was nothing exotic, that there was nothing in
my style of life to fascinate them. Jessica wasn't
disappointed.

My father wanted me to be a writer. He called it
being an author. Later, when he and I were no longer
friends, he couldn't have cared less what I did. But
at the beginning, when we were close, his eyes used
to light up and he'd grab me and say it would be a
grand life for me to become an author and that is
what I should set my heart on. He was dreaming he
was me. He used to take hold of me and say it and
then laugh and give me a hug, as if he really believed
it would happen. As if believing would make it
happen. He had no idea what he was talking about.
He was a hall porter in a club somewhere in London's west end, in Pall Mall or St James, one of those
places. He was a lackey. *Yes sir*, *Good morning sir*,

that sort of thing. His days and nights were filled with that stuff. He had to keep quiet about himself. That was as high as he ever reached, the outer hall. And it wasn't a matter of pride with him, but he just wasn't interested in the things the other hall porters were interested in. He didn't have a bet and he didn't follow the football. He was an eccentric, and in a hall porter that's sad. His own father had been lost in the North Sea, in a story that never made sense to me, a story that my father changed with his changing moods.

The idea of his son becoming an author was something to keep his spirits up. When he was old and had given up painting he started picking up second-hand books in the markets and spending his evenings at the dining table repairing their bindings. I never saw him read any of these books. These broken old books stood for something he'd never had. They stood for education. Intellectual freedom. Autonomy. That kind of thing. Refinement. The permission to lead another life. A better life. A secret life that had to be repaired and attended to. Himself in other words. The books stood for a quiet, disciplined, organised, productive life that he'd long ago despaired of. How could he put something like that together? In the end his despair came to fit exactly the volume of these old books. He'd had a terrible beginning in Glasgow. He died surrounded by hundreds of old books. My mother threw them out. She knew they weren't any good.

'Where are his books?' I asked her when I visited her after his death.

'I threw them out,' she said. 'I couldn't stand the smell. It was like having him still here.'

She'd repainted the place and hung new curtains at the windows. After her initial distress, his death was a release for my mother. Within a year she'd become one of those happy widows and he'd been all but forgotten.

'D'you miss Dad?' I asked her.

She gave me a look, a bit mischievous, and said, 'Well it's funny you know, but I don't.'

There are things that it's impossible to express with words. Language employed to express emotion is a perversion. The records of commerce is the only honest use of written language. The rest is a cover-up. It's not words that shape our intuitions. It's not in what we say but in what we leave unsaid that we reveal the shape of our deepest motives. In the places between the words. In the tacit and the implicit. In the silence beyond words. That's where we hide our truth. Behind the endless buzzing of language. The sovereignty of silence is its ambiguity. Silence is a power greater than speech.

It always begins with a question. An uncertainty. Then we become wanderers in search of ourselves. This affair of having a portrait painted. Jessica became at once flattered, insecure, vain, unsettled, resisting. She was all at a loss and went off warmed and glowing and scheming how she was going to influence the image of her that I was to bring into being. Not herself.

How it came about was this. Being at the university one day a week I met certain people I wouldn't otherwise have met and in this way was offered commissions I wouldn't otherwise have been offered. Within a week of running into her in the corridor on my way to the lift, I was offered a commission for a series of etchings to be published in a scholarly journal associated with the university. The job was the likenesses of ten eminent Australian women to accompany articles on their work and their careers. I got the offer over the phone and I turned it down flat. It didn't appeal to me. I didn't need the money. Once I would have grabbed it. But not any more. I wanted to recover. I was exhausted. But the editor of the journal forwarded the details to me through the post anyway.

Her name was on the list: Professor Jessica Keal, Visiting Fellow in the Department of History. I sat there on my high stool next to the solander in the studio staring at her name for several minutes, watching the two of us meeting in the empty corridor, watching a more responsive meeting than the real one had been. Then I made myself a cup of coffee and thought about it some more before ringing the editor of the journal and telling her I'd changed my mind and would accept the commission after all. But I hadn't really changed my mind about the likenesses. And as soon as I'd put the phone down I wished I hadn't rung the editor and I nearly rang her again to say I'd changed my mind back again. I thought of pretending someone had impersonated me the first time. I still didn't want to do the job. I knew what they'd be like, these eminent women. Likenesses. An invasion. And after all I wasn't sure. I didn't know whether I might have invented that little pool of trust just to comfort myself. That so-called offer. Maybe it hadn't really been there at all. Why *would* it have been there? No doubt she was just being polite. I didn't trust my memory of the event. We invent these things, we hope so hard for them, especially when we're tired and low in spirits and in need of reassurance that it hasn't all come to an end for us. We wake up in the middle of the night and we realise some little miracle has been offered to us during the day. And when it gets light we don't trust the miracle any more, and we decide we must have imagined it. We know this kind of hope can disable us.

So I'm sitting here on my stool with my pad held out at an angle, resting it on my knees, and I'm doing maybe my twentieth drawing of her. As I finish a drawing I flip the page over and begin a new one. I'm working quickly. She's sitting across from me on a straight-backed kitchen chair with the vertical lines of the stacks behind her, and she's facing the big verandah windows and looking out into my garden. She's wearing an open-necked shirt and jeans. 'What should I wear?' she asked over the phone. It's windy and the light is moving back and forth across her face from the movement of the foliage of the almond tree. I asked her at the beginning of the session if she'd keep perfectly still just for a little while. Now she's frozen into a profile. It amuses me, this anxiety on her own behalf. She doesn't want to risk me getting it wrong. Her vanity's involved. I know she's not going to look my way and I grimace at her. After a while I ask her to come around and face me. 'Look straight at me, Jessica,' I say. 'A visiting fellow in history. What kind of history?'

She starts telling me what she does. But I'm not following what she's saying. It doesn't make any sense to me. Her voice is just a background, something to let her move a bit, with her thoughts and her search for the words. She's started thinking about history and has forgotten to look her best. This is our first meeting. I've taken the likenesses of the other nine women. She's the last. I don't muck around with things like this. I grab as much information as I can in one sitting and that's that. My idea with likenesses is always to get the thing done and to move on to something else. There's always enough from one session for me to do a passable etching or a linocut. And that's what I do. I keep it brief.

I've nearly finished. She's been here three hours. An hour longer than any of the others had. We took a break for coffee. While I was getting our coffee she had a bit of a look around the studio, respectful, keeping her distance. And that was it. There's no sense of anything going on between us. There's this decision of restraint. Just two professional people getting on with the thing they have to do. That's the way we're doing it. But there's an edginess, as if there might be something else that we're *not* dealing with. I can't be sure whether I'm imagining this. It's hard to know. No doubt it's something to do with the delicate physics of desire, which can just as easily become the physics of boredom or revulsion.

I stop drawing and say, 'Thanks Jessica. That's it,' and I close the pad and put it on the solander behind me. Businesslike. I'm a busy man. We're both busy people. We don't want to waste each other's time. She gets off the stool and stretches and comes over and asks me, 'Can I have a look?'

I pick up the pad and turn it over, face down. She waits for me to offer it to her. She's not sure of me. She's tense. Then it dawns on her.

'Aren't you going to let me see?'

She's a bit incredulous. Her colour has heightened. Her eyes are dark brown and steady and she's looking at me as if she's wondering whether I'm a reasonable man or some kind of crank.

'There's nothing to see yet,' I say. I don't really know anything about her. I've finished getting my information for the likeness. That's all it's going to be, a likeness. I don't know the first thing about her. I know less about her now than I did when I walked into the common room where they were having the welcome for her and she looked across the room and we saw each other for the first time. In a way we knew everything about each other then. Now we know nothing. She'll be out of the studio in a minute and that'll be that. I might go on having regrets for ever. We'll nod to each other if we meet in the corridor. 'Hi,' we'll say. 'How's it going?' And there'll be that awkwardness between us because nothing was ever said.

I put the pad of drawings in the solander and close the drawer.

She stands in front of me and challenges me. 'Why won't you let me have a look?'

She's disappointed. She's angry with me. She's eager to see what I've done. She thinks she's been patient and deserves to have a look. That's *why* she's been patient, so she can claim her likeness from me at the end of the session. And there's her vanity. What have I seen, she's wondering? The likenesses are hers, that's what she thinks. She'd be confused, she might even feel misrepresented, if she saw what I've done. I've taken something from her, however, there's no getting away from that, and I've tucked it away in my solander out of her reach, in a place that's private to me. Her likeness. She's looking at me hoping I'll relent. I can feel how closed my features have become. Not that I mean to be this closed. It's just the way I am. It's being an artist that's done it. Keeping things to myself in case they lose their charge. So I close off. Especially when I'm working. I can't help it. I wish I could be light and open and friendly. But I can't do that.

She's seen it's no use trying to be angry with someone she doesn't know and who is this closed. She sees that anger's not going to work. And I watch her beginning to slide away with this realisation, going away completely, becoming unknown, making up her mind, her small anger turning towards dislike instead of disappointment. She's beginning to believe she's been mistaken about me.

'Well,' she says, and she smiles, a stiff little smile that suggests the possibility of contempt. 'Thanks. It was interesting.'

She's leaving. I'm following her down the steps

from the verandah into the garden. She's on the path and I'm still on the middle step when I say, 'I'd like to paint your portrait sometime, Jessica.'

I'm looking down at her. She turns abruptly and looks up at me, my words catching her. She's completely thrown. We look at each other. A big question is in her eyes. It might be too late. Then she looks away, her hand seeking the rail, slipping over the weathered timber, her fingertips lingering against the open grain, both of us looking at her hand, at her fingers playing over the surface of the weathered timber.

I see she knows that a portrait means something big and different and difficult. That it will not be easy. I see she knows that a portrait may fail. That it might be a project between us that fails. *Sometime* I said, so the thing's not certain. It hasn't been locked down. But she's been taken off-guard. She's flattered. She's confused now. Her vanity's been brought into it again. It's not over yet. It's unsettled her and something in her wants to resist the whole business. But she's already standing a little straighter, beginning to re-imagine herself in her own likeness, testing the thing out, preparing herself, watching a new visualisation of herself coming into being. A full portrait.

She's unsteadied. She's seeing all the portraits she's ever seen and she's wondering which one will be her. And she's not sure whether she wants to accept these possibilities.

'A portrait,' she says, as if this is something she has never considered before. 'How long will it take?' She looks concerned as she says this so that I won't notice that she's flattered. So that I'll think she's worried about finding the time in her busy life to sit for a portrait. She's pretending not to have understood anything, pretending she doesn't understand and may not be able to spare her attention for this kind of thing, pretending there's something here that only a painter would understand about a portrait.

'I don't do one picture,' I say. 'I do several.' It's a warning. I don't want her to get the wrong idea. 'Hundreds maybe. Some small, some not so small. And a few big ones. And drawings and etchings and woodcuts. Whatever I need. Photographs. I never know what I'm going to do. I keep several paintings on the go at once.'

She smiles at this, as if I might be teasing her, looking up at me, allowing herself to hope a little that maybe there's something after all. And I laugh. 'It's like that,' I say. 'It might take a year. Two years.

Who knows?' A portrait has never taken me two years and I say this knowing it to be a lie. I don't mean to mislead her. But I find myself lying to her, freely, as if I'm describing something I believe in. I'm describing the future. I don't know this at the time, of course, but that's what I'm doing, describing my future practice.

Suddenly she says, surprised and offering an apology, 'I've left my bag in your studio.'

'Your cigarettes are in it,' I say.

Everyone has to satisfy their curiosity about the image. They can't help themselves. If you're writing they don't take any notice of you. If you're writing they leave you alone. But if you're drawing they have to come and have a look over your shoulder. It's got something to do with the difference between the image and the word. The image is more primitive, it's more archaic and more direct and more public than the word. The image belongs to everyone. You can't keep it private. It jumps at us from ten thousand years ago from rock shelters in Arnhem Land and caves in Europe and from billboards on the side of the highway. When we see a drawing we all think we know what we're looking at. But the word is private. It's harder to get at. We're prepared to be puzzled. The word is more of a secret sign than the image. Antique inscriptions mean nothing to us. We need the genius of Champollion to decipher the Rosetta Stone for us, specialist knowledge, before we get anywhere near the meaning of the word. And it's a delicate matter. Words are not firmly attached to their meanings. If we're clumsy and push them too hard their meaning slips out and we're left with the husk. The empty sign. If we're writing it could be our diary or a love letter or a shopping list and it's no one's business but our own, but if we're drawing it's a matter for public concern. Jessica couldn't understand at first that these preparations belonged to me and were private. If I'd let her see them they'd have changed. They would have become something between us. I didn't try to explain. Then I surprised myself. I threw her the idea of a portrait before I'd had time to consider what I was saying. And when she'd got her bag and we were back in the studio, the wind whipping through the open door and making her hair blow around her face, she agreed.

I had a view of my garden through the large windows that enclosed the verandah. I'd let the garden grow wild. The previous owners had planted fruit trees. Apples and pears and plums. And the almond tree. So there was this neglected orchard outside my windows where the birds came in the autumn to eat the fruit. Down the hill were the tall Lombardy poplars bordering the reserve, and then the old gum trees they'd left standing.

No one who has a choice chooses to live in Canberra. I'm no exception. I didn't choose to live in Canberra but I had long ago decided that I'd probably never move away. My wife had been with the Department of Foreign Affairs. That's why we moved to Canberra in the first place. I was the one who'd stayed. Our son grew up there.

After Jessica Keal had gone that day I stood by the window looking into the garden for a long time. I didn't know what to think. I didn't know why I'd told her I wanted to do her portrait. It was a hot summer afternoon and I could hear children screaming down at the reserve. My house was quieter than usual and the garden emptier. I felt I might be making it all up between us. Just inventing something out of desperation. I was tired. My work was going through a stale patch and I wondered where I was going to get the energy from for this portrait. Even then, however, I detected a kind of intuitive stubbornness in myself about it, a dumb, inarticulate resolution at a great depth, which said there were no arguments and that I was going to go through with her portrait no matter what. This was really the first inkling I had that she was going to change things for me.

My father's gone of course. Long ago. My mother too now. There's no one left. They may as well not have existed. My family. It all came to nothing for them. All the passions and hopes and the little dreams and wayward moments. The small repair jobs. It was a piece of music performed once and never repeated. My family. My family history. My life. My life story. I could hardly remember how it went. Now and then a couple of bars would come into my head and I'd struggle to link them up with a larger theme. Something magisterial, grand, portentous, something with a bit of authority and romance in it. But there was nothing. No theme. No sweeping gesture across the homeland. It had left no trace. Hardly any. He said to me one day, 'That girl came to visit us after you left. Did you know that?'

He was still accusing me of something after all those years had gone by. Twenty years. And it was related to sex, of course, sex that he'd never had and that I'd had. He was still thinking about it. Still nursing this little injury, this grudge. It was long after we'd ceased to be friends. I was living over in Paris at the time, visiting the art museums, and my mother was off on a trip to Spain with my sister and her husband. My sister was paying for the trip. It was my mother's first holiday outside England. They'd invited him too. But my father had refused to go with them.

While I was over there in Paris enjoying myself I thought of him alone in our old council flat in London. I hadn't paid a visit for nearly ten years. So I went over to see him. I probably had some nostalgic illusion about it. The old place. Home.

I was nervous about seeing him. It wasn't nothing to me. It wasn't easy for me to visit him.

He was drinking watered whisky from a tumbler like the one he'd kept his teeth in on the bathroom shelf when I was a kid. And he was attending to his books, the kitchen table littered with bits and pieces of material and this odd sort of repair kit of tools he'd put together for himself, pretending he was a craftsman. He didn't offer me a drink. Other men his age were out looking after their allotments or putting on a bet, which was the kind of thing he despised more than anything. Gardening, gambling, the ordinary things. He'd never had a friend. He made no pretence of welcoming me. He didn't want to see me. It was as simple as that. He wanted to be left alone.

He's got his glasses on the end of his nose and his hat on to keep his head warm and he's bent over the table dabbing oil or glue or something on the spine of a book. I'm standing there watching him and wishing I hadn't come over, when he says, quiet and intent on dabbing at the book, 'That girl came to see us you know.' And there's a pause while he goes on dabbing and I register that he's said something to me.

'What girl?' I say.

He looks up at me, just a quick assessment, his eye gleaming out from under the brim of his hat, and he adjusts his glasses with his finger and sniffs. I understand something I've never understood before. He hates me. There's a small cold place in my chest where I realise this. It's something that's just grown in him over the years. Maybe he's only just realised it himself. It's not his fault. It's a tumour. A tumour of hatred. It will kill him. He doesn't want it treated. He doesn't want to recover from it. He wants me to know I'm killing him. He wants the tumour of hatred to kill him. He wants me to know that all the time I've been living in Australia, ever since I emigrated on my own as a boy, ever since I escaped, that I've been killing him. He blames me. His son. Who else? For the failure of those old dreams. The enormous tumour he carries is my fault. Now I've come back to have a look at him and he doesn't want me to see him. It only makes things worse. I'm spoiling his party. His private party with these old books and the whisky and his paraphernalia. I'm looking into his secret, and it's empty, and he doesn't know how to defend its emptiness from the destruction of my gaze.

'What girl?' I ask him. Even though I'm remembering. There was only one. I'm incredulous. I've realised what he's talking about. It's twenty years ago. He dabs at the book and while he waits for the glue to season he rolls one of his cigarettes and sniffs a couple more times. He's satisfying his hatred of his son.

'She sat over there,' he says, licking the cigarette paper and pointing over his glasses towards the gas fire.

'Your mother gave her a cup of tea.'

His smell is sour. Rancid. He's like some leftover

shoved to the back of the pantry and forgotten. Where's the lovely aromatic walnut and paints and sharpened pencils now?

I was fifteen and she was eighteen. I'd left school and was working for a farmer in Somerset, in a village near the edge of Exmoor, before emigrating to Australia. She worked with her mother in the late-night sandwich caravan at the bus station in Taunton. That's how I met her. I'd started going in to Taunton on a Saturday afternoon to look for a bit of relief. I'd go to the pictures then hang around the Blue Dolphin watching the loving couples. Then I'd catch the last bus back to the farm.

Except for one or two stragglers like me the bus station was deserted at that time of night. There was just this van where you could get a ham sandwich and a cup of tea. I sat out in the dark in one of the shelters and watched her. It was a little drama. A private theatre. She and her mother in the lighted van serving the stragglers, framed by the enormous dark allotment of the deserted bus station. I'd go to the bus station early just to watch her. Her fresh white apron over her blouse and her bare arms, her dark hair loose over her shoulders, tossing back and forth as she worked, its lights going this way and that, fascinating me. The way her mother glanced sideways at her, proud and afraid. Stern and yielding. I'd think about her all week while I was working on the farm and on Saturday afternoon I'd have a bath in front of the stove and dress up in my suit and catch the bus to town. And there she would be. The tea and sandwich girl.

Before I spoke she'd sensed my fear. She laughed and looked triumphantly at her mother. The cool night and the rain. Our poverty, which we were not aware of, and which was as pure as our youth. We were innocent and cruel. The enormous night. Our bodies. I don't remember the sequence. Maybe there wasn't a sequence. Maybe you forget these passages the way you forget the seconds immediately before an accident. I can hardly see into it now. When I was to emigrate to Australia and had returned to London, I told my father I was going back to Taunton for my last weekend. He said, 'You're not leaving some girl in trouble are you?'

I scoffed at such a possibility. But he knew. We were having a beer together. Men. For the first and last time in our lives. I wanted him to give me one of his old-fashioned hugs and to see his eyes light up with possibilities for me before I went. But he'd stopped dreaming he was me.

'I'm going to say goodbye to my friends,' I told him, swallowing the beer he'd bought me.

'What friends?' he wants to know. It's his turn to scoff. 'I've never heard you talk about any friends.' He warns me then against causing suffering. He's serious about this. It's a lecture. He wants his son to be a good man. A decent man. Moral and upright. As he has never been able to be himself but has always wished to be. We're standing at the bar in the railway station and we both know I'm only going back for one thing. There's a disgust and a hopelessness with this knowledge between us that has never been there before. It establishes our lives. Our futures. We see how sordid we are. We've both failed already. The little dream of childhood gone. His and mine. We can't admire each other. It's all over. And when I leave to catch the train we shake hands and avoid each other's eyes. The seed of his tumour has already germinated. I feel the weight that it will grow to in twenty years as I walk away from him down the platform.

I'm excited by her tears. Her nakedness. The way she lies on the bed with her back to me, curled away from me, curled into herself and into her despair, her bare thighs glistening in the blue light from the street and the rain. My power to abandon her increasing me, oppressing me. I reach out and touch her shoulder. I am lost. I feel my loneliness for the first time in my life. I am longing to be my old self.

'I'll come back in two years,' I promise softly, thrilling to the lie. Her dark hair is filled with unusual light. She is my first woman. I hadn't expected this. The slowness and the gravity. I can't wait to be gone and to have her complete, as my memory. Light and safe. I promise to write from Australia's outback. She clings to me when I try to leave and weeps, promising a life, vowing it, like a knight-errant vowing fidelity to a sovereign, faithful until death. Her humiliation is so compelling I almost decide to stay.

I get dressed and go out the door and down the stairs and I leave the house where she has her room. I am a meaner and a grander version of my old self. I no longer know what I am, or what I am to become. I am grown and diminished. And as I walk away, suddenly her insults and her hatred are streaming after me into the darkness. Gratifying me. Lashing the air.

A storm beating down on me. Making me duck and run. I'm being cursed. I become a man with a curse on me. It never leaves me in all the years I wander around Australia. It never leaves any of us. The curse. God's curse. Damn you! Damn you! Damn you! Three times to make it stick. And we deserve it.

'That's right,' my father says, dragging out his message, dragging on his pungent cigarette, inspecting with the cracked tips of his fingers the state of the glue, the repair he's making to the spine of the worth-less book, then gesturing at the room he's lived in for fifty years. 'She came here to see us and sat over there and your mother gave her a cup of tea.'

He is merciless and without dignity.

I remind him, 'Remember when we used to go on the Greenline bus and paint, Dad? Out into the country?'

'We went *once*!' he shouts. His truth denies every-thing. I've betrayed him. He is already mad. He wishes to remind me. He has possessed no influence with me. She came to see them. She was eighteen. I'll never remember her name. She had no existence except my existence. I remember only her nakedness, cool and pale and glowing on the bed, as I leave. She's still with me. There's the guilt, the secret joyful guilt, and there's this faint arousal, like an old song carried to me then lost.

Jessica brought me some family snapshots. 'That's all there are,' she said. They were in an old tin from her mother's place. There were one or two letters and some postcards in the tin as well as the snapshots. The postcards were from her from London, addressed to her mother in the Araluen Valley. I pinned the photos on the wall above the solander and we looked at them. A proof of the etching I'd done for the journal was lying on the solander. While I pinned up the photos she examined the proof, turning it round in her hands, holding it off, squinting at it, trying it this way then that way.

'Do you like it?' I asked, observing her, wanting her to like it. It was the first time an artist had taken her likeness. She didn't know what to think. It disturbed her to see this image that was her and not her. Seeing herself as strange, flat and familiar for the first time. Disquieted by the little gulf of detachment opened for her by the print. The printed drawing. The intimate sign of my hand moving across the page. A touch she'd scarcely felt. A reproduction. Once removed. Twice removed. She didn't know how to approach it. Screwing up her face in an effort to *see* into the likeness a feeling of herself in there. The two-dimensional image calling her in and warding her off at the same time. The likeness getting in the way of seeing anything at all. Nothing to see. The likeness being unforgiving, revealing everything. Concealing everything. Her eyes were like cold discs. It was another woman. She wanted to ask me if I really saw her this way, if people, if *everyone*, saw this woman when they saw *her*. But she held back the question and kept it to herself. I watched her.

She turned to me. 'Perhaps you get used to it.'

'It's only a likeness,' I said, and I took it out of her hand and slipped it into the drawer.

Portraiture is the art of misrepresentation. It's the art of unlikeness. That's why it's so difficult. No one really knows how to do it. It's all guesswork. You've got to avoid the authority of the likeness. You can't afford to be trapped by that. You've got to slip past the likeness and close your eyes to it. You've got to reach into the dark and touch something else. The problem is always to visualise the person. Portraiture is an act of faith. In portraiture it's the shy beast you're after not the mask. Beauty and the Beast. You've got to entice the beast out of hiding into the open, past the gentle contours of the familiar. You've got to be patient and wait till it makes a move. If you rush things you'll scare it and it'll never come out. You have to gain its trust. You have to put yourself in danger. You have to offer it something of yourself. You have to take a risk.

That's not the whole truth, of course.

Portraiture's a dangerous business. It's fraught with misunderstanding. I slipped the etching into the drawer. I didn't offer to give her an impression. I didn't want her likeness coming between us. That's the mistake we make, to look for the perfect image. That's Greek philosophy. It's the antique error. The error of monotheism. It gets you nowhere. The longing for a fixed truth resident behind the reality we've brought into being ourselves. That's futility. The fallacy of the Western intellectual tradition, the idea of perfection. As if our reality is going to hold forever, in there somewhere if only we can get to it, if only we can dig deep enough, a hard impermeable kernel of truth that will hold out against the apocalypse of our loss of faith.

I closed the drawer. 'It's the signature they want

from me these days,' I said. 'Likenesses are all alike.'

She wasn't sure whether I was mocking her or not. That's how careful you have to be. You have to think before you speak. It takes two to make a portrait. And one of them's always yourself.

She's a fourth generation Australian. She tells me this as if it's something for her to be proud of, something she's required to feel modest about. Four generations, her gaze looking off into the past as she says it. Her ancestors came from Devon. But first she tells me her mother lives in the Araluen Valley. I'd heard of the Araluen Valley but had never been there. It's two hours drive. People in Canberra often spoke to me of the Araluen Valley. They always said how beautiful it was, as if they owned it, or as if it owed its beauty to their appreciation of it, as if knowing *about* it made them superior to me for not knowing about it. Being able to tell me about it confirmed them in their good opinion of themselves. As if they were responsible for the beauty they were acknowledging. So it had never occurred to me to go to the Araluen Valley.

'Have you been to the Araluen Valley?' It's the first question I'd ask whenever there was an overseas visitor around. I'd get in before the others had a chance. 'You'd better go there,' I'd say. 'It's not to be missed!'

Her mother's place is not exactly in the Araluen Valley. It's several kilometres past the main part of the valley, where the peach orchards are — which is the part that everyone knows and has told me about, the beautiful part, the picturesque part. Her mother's place is further down the Araluen Creek towards the coast, where the valley closes in and the road winds along up on the side of the hill through the forest, it's down towards the junction with the river. Her mother's place is concealed from the road by the stringy-bark forest. You wouldn't know it was there if you were driving past along the road. We have to take a side-road through the forest to get to it. Here we're among the underbrush and dry ground-cover. Then we come out onto a slope covered with thin native grass, a small paddock that runs down towards an unpainted split slab and weatherboard house surrounded by a fenced garden. Beyond the house there's a couple of outbuildings then a sense of a steep bank and a creek. Casuarinas rise above the line of the roof of the house and the outbuildings, their foliage light and moving, the sky behind them glinting as the breeze moves them back and forth. The light of the day is sharp and clear. The grass and the trees shine with it. The surface of the close-cropped paddock is polished. A wisp of silver smoke rises from the chimney at the far end of the house. A woman is in the garden, bent over, chipping at something. Beyond the house and the garden and beyond the creek and the casuarinas, hills close off the distance, soft with the forest. Magpies walk about near the perimeter of the garden and stab at the ground for insects. They pause in their search to examine us, and they warble in a quiet, interior way, conversing with themselves. When we pull up, the woman in the garden continues to chip at the earth. She hasn't heard us.

Jessica switches off the motor and we sit in the car. It's as if she's made a decision. As if she's arrived at a decision to stay in the car. It's possible we won't be getting out of the car. It's possible she'll give me a look at the old place from where we are then drive back out to the road again, like strangers who've taken a minute to decide they've driven into the wrong place. I can hear her breathing. I can feel her uncertainty, her tension after the long drive.

Then she says, 'The Keal place.'

Presenting it to me.

'I don't know why you had to see it. It isn't me any more.' She makes an impatient noise in her throat, acknowledging that she's never going to find the words to explain the significance of this place to me. Or to herself. On the drive down she's told me her story. It's a kind of reverse of my own story, though I haven't remarked on this because her telling is complicated by certain other things, and because to have mentioned myself would have been to deflect her from her own story, which I was eager to hear. She left this place on a scholarship when she was eighteen and went to live in London. She was, she says, the only person from Lower Araluen to ever do this. In the valley it gives her the distinction of someone who sold out. A traitor. A renegade.

'They don't get over that,' she says. 'They don't forget that kind of thing in a hurry.' What's thirty years, after all, when you're talking about four or five generations? But they might, she suggests, boast about her going to London even though they'll make her pay for it. She's given them a certain distinction. She's lived in England for thirty-one years and she's become a distinguished professor. Now she's a visiting fellow at the National University. But as far as they're concerned she's still accountable to them. I understand

43

that *them* really refers to her mother. She still has responsibilities in the valley. It's her birthright.

She's not sure whether she's come back to live in Australia or not. She doesn't say this. It's something I gather for myself. Something I get a feeling about. She says definitely she has no plans to stay in Australia beyond the end of the year, when her visiting fellowship will come to an end. But I don't feel convinced about this. She would like, she says, to see that her mother is properly cared for. That some arrangement is made, before she goes back. That's all. But she's not detailed about this. There's some concealed difficulty that she doesn't speak of to me. She is troubled about the whole business and for some reason to hear this in her voice makes me feel very close to her. This is the feeling on the way down in the car. Being a passenger and going somewhere new and listening to her. The magic of the drive has come to an end now that we've arrived. I feel a little let down and try not to show it.

'It's very beautiful,' I say. 'Very peaceful and beautiful.'

'Yes,' she says, drawling the word, as if she's reluctant to agree but can see no alternative. And she gets out her cigarettes and shakes one from the packet.

We're both wondering if this project of the portrait will go ahead or whether it'll fizzle out. We don't know yet. It could go either way. We're not making any rash forecasts. But it has complicated things for both of us and we're not sure that we need the complication. Maybe we don't have the energy for it. Maybe it's too late for this kind of thing. We sit in the car and watch the woman in the garden. Her mother. The sun is warm coming through the closed windows of the car. I convince myself not to worry about anything and soon begin to enjoy the feeling of being in the country. Of not working and being on an outing and not having the responsibility of being the one who's in charge. It's more complicated for her, I tell myself, than it is for me. There's the click and scrape of a steel hoe against stones and the faint shrieking of insects.

'You'd think nothing's changed,' she says quietly, as if she's had to say this. The very least she could say with all the things that must be going around in her head. Her entire childhood. The peace and quiet of an autumn morning in the country.

'There used to be a lot of families around here. All through the bush. There were people all through this area. There was a school.' Her schoolgirl friends running down the hill with her, swinging their bags and yelling and her mother coming from the garden to greet them, and going into the little house and giving them milk and biscuits, or whatever she had for the occasion. I remember my own big chunks of fresh crusty bread-and-dripping after school, the dripping scraped from the bottom of the bowl with the dark sauce in it, and lots of pepper and salt.

'My mother's the last of them. She's the last of the old people. The others are all dead.'

She turns to me after she says this, potentially hostile, appraising me. Wanting me to be more responsive. I've been making noises of assent. Trying to sound interested. Am I worth these painful disclosures? Someone who does not communicate in volumes of words. Is there any point in giving me this information? I don't say anything. I can't think of anything to say. I look out at what she's talking about. I'm looking at her old home. The place she grew up in. There's a broken post-and-rail fence running along-side us. It's been fixed with barbed wire years ago, then the barbed wire's rusted and broken and a couple of steel posts have been driven in and some plain wire strung along. The whole thing's just hanging there, ready to fall over. There are three white-faced cows in the paddock lying in the shade of a big tree and watching us, their heads rocking from side to side, chewing and chasing off the flies. They don't look as though they're going to challenge the fence. I can think of nothing to say. I regret my silence but can do nothing about it. It's the lines of my drawing, thin and spindly, like my writing, meagre and secretive. Messages to myself. A deep habit. Cagey, tight and cryptic. My art began as a private listening device for detecting something out there in the silence that would keep me interested. Fragments. I learned to look for fragments, not for whole things.

She turns to me and, smiling, asks me what I'm thinking. She's been distracted from her own thoughts. I realise I've probably sighed.

She touches my shoulder and swivels round in her seat and points behind us. 'See that walnut tree up the hill there?' It's March and the air is bright with the first touch of autumn. The enormous tree is heavy with clusters of green nuts. 'My grandmother and her mother are buried under that tree,' she says. 'My great-grandmother planted it. My mother buried my grandmother there when I was a girl.'

I twist around in my seat and look up the hill at the tree, awkwardly craning around to see it through the

47

rear window, trying to absorb the density of the history that's being offered to me, the significance of all this. Jessica's watching me.

'My mother wants me to bury her there,' she says and waits for me to look at her. 'It's one of the things she's expecting from me.'

'Do they still allow you to do that?'

'Well, we'll see. Shall we get out?' she says and laughs. We both laugh. And for a moment we like each other in a way that is open and without complication.

'My father used to keep his paints in a walnut box,' I tell her. 'We went out into the country every weekend together to paint.' We get out of the car and she lights her cigarette and we walk up the hill to have a look at the walnut tree and her ancestral graves.

'You've been a painter all your life then?'

My success as an artist came with the sale of the *Tan Family* portrait to MOMA, which everyone has heard of. It wasn't until I was successful that I seriously began to doubt my ability. When I was working on the *Tan Family* portrait I felt the necessity of it. That piece of work had singled me out. Which is the nearest thing to inspiration. The knowledge of its necessity is the inspiration of a work. That's what I'm hoping for with Jessica. It's what I'm always hoping for. I know it's not a free gift. I haven't had it for a long time and I'm hoping to get beyond the uncertain stage with this project. So far there's still only this mute stubbornness.

She's sitting on a narrow iron bed in a room that's so small she could nearly touch both walls if she were to stretch out her arms. She's looking out of the window. Only you can't see the window. But that's where the light's coming from. The window is off the frame to the left. It's her old bed from when she was a child. She's in her old bedroom in her mother's house. She's being assailed by the sounds and smells of her child-hood home. Nothing *has* changed. She's looking out the window at her mother hoeing in the garden. The click and scrape of her mother's hoe on the stony ground. Whenever she sits here looking out the window at her silent mother in the garden, Jessica tells me, she feels that her journey back to Lower Araluen has been a mistake. Once she is actually here, in this place where she grew up, with the smells and old familiar sounds, once she can see and can touch the broken and the worn and the cared-for bits and pieces of this place, she begins to feel that by returning she has willed some kind of punishment on herself. There's a heaviness in being in her mother's house that she can't explain or shift from her mood. 'I hadn't expected to feel at home,' she says. 'The difficulties, I mean, of being at home.'

She tries to talk to me about this when we're in Canberra at my place and I'm drawing her. Sitting by the big windows in the studio she tries to tell me about it.

'My mother in the garden, hoeing the earth the way she's always hoed the earth,' she says, speaking her thought suddenly into the quiet room with just my scratching on the pad with the stub of charcoal. 'It's her own earth. She's the one who's created it! The rest of that hill's just rock.' She takes a packet of cigarettes from her bag and shifts it about in her hands, feeling its edges with her thumb.

'I don't mind,' I tell her. 'It's okay. Have a cigarette if you want.'

She thanks me and strokes her bag. The bag is a fine green leather. 'I bought this bag in Florence last summer,' she says, stroking the bag, as if it's a pet on her knees. She looks at me and laughs as she lights her cigarette. 'I should give them up,' she says. 'I keep meaning to.' She closes her eyes and lets the smoke drift from her lips. For a moment she looks young. The person she once was.

In her childhood bedroom in her mother's house at Lower Araluen there's a little blue china dish on the chest of drawers. The room is so small that Jessica doesn't need to get up from the bed in order to reach the dish. The little dish fits snugly into the palm of her hand. She taps the ash from her cigarette into the little blue dish, which she remembers from when she was a child, and she weeps. It's the first moment of her return. As the tears run down her cheeks she lifts her face to the ceiling and blows out the smoke of her cigarette. It is a confusion that is both sadness and joy that makes her weep. Then she stubs out her cigarette and she dries her eyes and blows her nose. And she replaces the blue china dish on the chest of drawers and she laughs and tells herself that she is an idiot. She runs her hand along the top of the chest of drawers. A piece, like a small bite taken from a pie, is broken from the bevelled edge of the chest of drawers. She inserts the ball of her thumb into the hollow of the 'bite' and rubs it back and forth. This is one of those idle gestures that are ventured upon involuntarily. There is something intensely familiar, something unexpectedly private and deeply personal, in the pleasure she gets from the feeling of rolling the ball of her thumb in the hollow of the wood. She is taken by surprise and she repeats the action. She rolls the ball of her thumb in the little hollow and searches in her memory for something. But it is like trying to remember a dream after waking. The harder she tries to remember, the more recessed the image becomes, until it is lost altogether. She stands by the bed looking at the chest of drawers and she feels suddenly heavy and old, and she wishes she were back in England and could call her friend, Caroline, and have a laugh and be on confident ground again in the present. She wishes she hadn't come back to Australia, to the valley. She wishes she had left it all in her memory. She wishes she had neglected her mother and the whole issue of the possibility of a return. She tells me, 'I'm not one of those people who insist that there can never be any regrets in their past. I think that's just cowardly,' she says.

She crosses her legs and she leans her elbow on her knee. She inspects me keenly and draws on her cigarette and she tells me that she misses her friend. 'I miss her, Caroline,' she says, savouring the pain of saying her absent friend's name aloud. 'Should I chuck this in and just go back?' she asks me. 'What do you think? Tell me honestly what you think. Should I call it a day?'

I turn the page and begin another drawing. 'Stay like that,' I say. 'Leaning forward, just as you are.' Her eyes are narrowed against the smoke of her cigarette and her face is tilted up towards me and she's examining me, finding me worthy of these questions, looking into her feelings for me. The soft afternoon light from the window is falling across her cheek, and she is wondering about things in her life, and just for this moment, for no reason, she is suddenly happy. Through her sadness she is happy. I would like to tell her that she is beautiful. But it is better to say nothing and to hope that I will gather the charge of this story into my images by remaining silent. She waits for me. Watching me. There is a sensuousness in being told to stay as she is. There is enjoyment in it. I feel her gaze on my face as I draw.

She's wearing a brooch pinned to the v of her blouse. It's a replica of an antique Celtic design, a gold circlet set with paste and amber and blue. I admired it earlier when she arrived. Now, while I draw her, she fingers the brooch and reminds me that I admired it and she tells me this story about it. I feel there's a reason for her telling me the story, but I don't know what the reason is. Perhaps she just wants to talk about her friend. Who knows? It's guesswork. It's all guesswork. Maybe she doesn't know the reason herself. But still, I have this feeling she's telling me something else while she's telling me the story of how she came by the brooch.

'Caroline gave it to me,' she says, reaching for the brooch and touching it with the tips of her fingers, the way a blind person might, forming its shape in her mind. 'We had dinner together the night before I left. It was an Indian restaurant in Beaconsfield. Do you know Beaconsfield? It was London you were from wasn't it? It had belonged to her mother. Her mother used to wear it all the time. Caroline's mother and I were friends. When she died I missed her more than Caroline did. *I feel free*, Caroline said to me when the news of her mother's death came through. But that wasn't how *I* felt. It was a generous gift. We spent a few minutes admiring it. When I went to fix it to my dress the hasp broke and it fell from my hands in two pieces. I couldn't say anything. I felt it must be an omen. Caroline just looked at me, as if she blamed me. As if I'd broken her gift on purpose. I couldn't defend myself. Caroline's mother and I had shared a particular understanding that for a number of reasons I'd never been able to talk about to Caroline. Her mother had helped me a lot in the early days. So when Caroline gave me the brooch I was secretly a bit embarrassed. It was a shock to see the brooch. I mean I had to pretend I felt something simple when really I had this rush of memories. It was as if her mother was giving me the brooch through Caroline. So when it broke I felt that the more complicated side of the gift was being exposed. Are you superstitious? Isn't everybody? I picked up the pieces of the brooch and I was thinking about my own mother. I was thinking about this business of coming back to Australia and seeing her again. I sat there in the restaurant with the two pieces of the brooch in my hand and I knew there was some sort of complicated connection with home and my mother and all that stuff I'd left behind thirty years ago and that I was going back to in the morning. I'm wearing it now in defiance of those feelings. Do you know what I mean? Do you understand that? We both drank quite a bit that night. We couldn't shake off the feeling of hostility between us. Caroline is taller than me. She's very thin and younger than I am. She's English and she can seem to be disapproving in a very glassy impenetrable way, as if you've transgressed some basic rule that you're never going to understand and that doing this has let her down. She can't be made to talk about it. She's even more disapproving if I try to talk about it. Sometimes I absolutely loath her and I can feel her loathing me. It's horrible. That's what it was like. But we persisted. We stayed on and drank Drambuie after the wine. The harder we tried the worse it got. The restaurant bill was enormous. I flinched when I saw it. We'd planned this celebration and she'd given me this generous gift and everything had fallen apart and I was leaving first thing in the morning to go to Australia for a year. I knew she was wishing there was some way she could take her mother's brooch back. We parted disliking each other. A jeweller in Sydney repaired the brooch while I waited. He said it was nothing and wouldn't charge me for it.'

Jessica stopped talking and looked down at the brooch and touched it. 'Caroline's mother gave it to me from the grave. It was difficult, but she did it. You must think this is all very stupid. I rang Caroline soon after I arrived and everything was all right between us. She asked me how the flight was. I didn't tell her I'd had the brooch repaired. We talked about the possibility of her coming out for a holiday. She said she'd think about it. She's my very best friend. I've known her since my first week in London. But there are still things I can't talk to her about.'

The big silvery redgum in the paddock beyond the garden where the white-faced cows are is acting as a reflector and is driving the light against the window. But the room's resisting the light. The room, this other room, her old bedroom down here at Lower Araluen, is staying in a kind of low suffused state of semi-darkness. Vertical blocks of deep purple and umber, the earth shadows, which contain their own resistant densities. Resisting the streaming light that's crashing against the side of the house and shaking the window, which is throwing it back. As if the air outside is filled with millions of fragments of exploded glass. The light hissing dangerously across the garden and the paddocks, and that faint dry shrieking all the time, which never stops, so that you cease to hear it and feel the irritation of the nerves, an abrasion of the senses, pervasive and deep and incurable, or, inexplicably you are soothed by it. It becomes a quality of the silence. And the old woman bent over tapping at the ground, tap, tap, tap, encompassed by the storm of light and noise that's raging all around her, probing for something in the earth with her iron implement. Engrossed.

It's a picture of a woman sitting on a bed looking out of a window. That's what the portrait is. It's only the second time I've done a portrait of someone in their bedroom. A bedroom portrait. The other one was Dr Henry Guston on his deathbed. *Henry*, as I called it, created a controversy with the Archibald committee. They couldn't decide whether a corpse was a proper subject for portraiture. But as there was nothing in the rules disqualifying cadavers they were forced to hang it. It didn't win of course. They accused me of trying to gain some notoriety with *Henry*. Which I didn't need as I'd already sold the *Tan Family* and everyone was trying to get something off me by then. I was painting money.

My portrait of Henry wasn't like Rembrandt's *Anatomy Lesson*. I mean I didn't begin it expecting to do a corpse. He was my friend. One of my very few friends. I've never had more than one or two friends in my entire life. I've never had the problem of too many friends. I know people who have that problem. They're always apologising for not seeing them. But Henry Guston was one friend I did have. I loved him. He and I fell into friendship years ago, when I first came to live in Canberra with my wife. He was at the CSIRO. It was like falling in love. I wanted to talk to everyone about him. It was recognition. It was believing. Henry was one of the nicest people I'd ever met. We didn't care what the other one did or how the other one lived. He wasn't like me. Henry knew how to live as well as how to work. Which I think is a rare gift. It was something I envied him. It was something I didn't know how to do. It's not something you learn. He had lots of friends. That was another gift, the gift of friendship. Henry was a gifted man. I was just one of his many friends. Which was fine. He knew how to make you feel okay about that kind of thing. Anyway he was fit and well and happy when I started working on his portrait. Then he died without warning. His death was completely unexpected. It was a great shock to me, to everyone. His wife and children were struck a terrible blow. Henry's death left me without a friend. I resented his death. I went round to his place in a fiercely resentful state of mind and stood by his bed, looking at his dead face, talking to him, telling him what I thought of him, gathering from his features certain information I couldn't resist and could never have found any other way. I had my little sketchbook and I made a few notes. I was careful to do it while there was no one else in the room. People get upset about these things. Those notes turned out to be the basis of the portrait.

No one liked the picture. None of Henry's other friends. And his wife wouldn't look at it. We've never spoken to each other since. She's not like Henry. Henry would have understood. And if he hadn't understood he would have forgiven me. They said it wasn't Henry. That it was too cold. Too grim and too austere. He'd never been like that, they said. Never. What did I think I was trying to do? Was this some kind of iconoclasm? If I'd thought of Henry like that why hadn't I had the courage to say so while he was alive? And so on. I defended myself. I said, 'That's how I saw him at the end.' They said I must be losing my touch, that I was falling away. But it was Henry who'd fallen away, not me. I never sold it. No one wanted it. It's hanging in my bedroom. I'm considering showing it to Jessica. But maybe it's too soon for that yet. She might take fright. She might wonder what I'm up to. I don't know what I'm up to. I'm guessing.

He's not lying in bed. He's sitting up. He's slipping sideways. He's falling away. Falling through the gauze curtains that were there to keep the mosquitoes off him. The likeness of a dead man. That's what confused them. The likeness. I should have provided them with a set of notes. I should have explained myself. I shouldn't have left things in that unexplained state. But that's what I do. It confuses people. They think I'm trying to be smart. They take offence. Who does he think he is? they want to know. It puts them off. But I don't have an explanation for them. I'd have to make one up. I'd have to invent something soothing. It wouldn't do any good. They'd argue back at me. An explanation from me would be an invitation to them to negotiate a new picture out of me. I'd never hear the end of it. *Can't you make him a bit warmer looking? I mean, Henry, for Christ's sake! You remember our Henry don't you?* An explanation wouldn't help. So I say nothing and they take my silence for arrogance.

Every now and then, after the lapse of a few minutes of stillness, an eddy of air sets the leaves of the big redgum in motion. The redgum is a tree Jessica remembers from her childhood. She had forgotten it. But now she remembers it. 'It looks just the same as it did when I was a child,' she tells me. 'That tree hasn't changed,' she says, marvelling. 'A branch or two has fallen off. That's all.'

It's an ancient tree, you can see that. It was here hundreds of years before the first Keal woman from Devon, her ancestor Amelia, knocked out the wattles and got this garden and these little paddocks of grazing going, while the men were off looking for gold in the valley and the women were taking care of food and shelter and the upbringing. And they've had their peculiar history, the Keal women and the garden, ever since, their eccentric story of persistence. Till Jessica's desertion. And when her mother dies that'll be the end of it. The tourists can move in and take over then. The tourists can discover the hidden beauties of Lower Araluen, the picturesque and the rustic, the few remains of another Australia that no one really belongs to any more, but which is still there, hanging on in places like this, and managing to believe in itself by dismissing everything else.

Every now and then an eddy of air sets the leaves of the redgum in motion and the light passes back and forth unsteadily across her features, the way light might pass mysteriously across the bed of a river, its hues diluted and made more lucid and slowed by the weight of the water. Back and forth, the shadow of someone's hand at the window. A gesture from outside. An invitation. A summons. Someone calling her out of herself. The leaves of the redgum hang down in great airy clusters from an enormous height and they bend back and forth in the warm eddies of air, glinting. Finely beaten tin.

Set in motion by the intermittent breeze, the leaves of the redgum are signalling.

When a bird cries once from a branch in the tree, then again, and abruptly falls silent, its cries set something new in motion in the room, in the mind of the woman who is sitting on the bed and to whom there has been this mysterious call from outside. The silence hangs during the interval after the bird's cry, waiting for her reply, until the bird calls again, now from farther away. The sound of the bird's call is being swallowed by distance and light as it flies further away from the house. It is becoming hollowed and echoing and more imaginary the further away it gets. It no longer calls for a reply. The cry of the bird is becoming part of the elaborate silence of the stringybark forest and of the woman's thoughts, her uncertainty, her inability to reply. As it grows more indistinct and imaginary, for the woman who is sitting on the bed the call of the bird becomes a kind of lamentation for what is lost and cannot be recovered. She might have followed the call of the bird. A cry in which there is also a note of mockery, which makes the woman on the bed a little afraid, which has made her hesitate. So that fear has begun to be present in the room. When the bird has retreated and merged into the distance and into memory there remains, in the darkened room with the woman, a stirring complicated silence that might be difficult for her to distinguish from the sound of her own blood. This is a silence of strain and fatigue and worry. It is an undifferentiated silence. It is a silence that is the opposite of calm, graceful or beautiful music, and is not just the absence of such music. It is a silence in which the woman's uncertainty, her diffidence, has begun to oppress her. Her failure to decide. To make a decision, the way she has been able to make decisions throughout her life. To perceive her direction. To leave when it is time to leave. To know these things. To exercise her will and her intuition, her sense of what is right for herself. Now it has become a dilemma. She is surprised and dismayed and she is thinking, *It has never happened to me before. Why am I like this?* And the click and scrape of the steel hoe against the stony ground is reminding her of her mother. To locate this sound from her childhood. To deal with it. Her mother at work in the garden.

Jessica's mother, Enid Keal, is a deeply silent woman. She has said nothing to indicate that Jessica isn't welcome. She's made no sign that she doesn't want Jessica around the place. But all the same, Jessica feels certain that her mother doesn't want her hanging around being a visitor. She's sure her mother feels as burdened and overwhelmed by these recurrent visits to the valley, after all this time of absence, as she feels herself. But she can't talk to her mother about this. Her mother, she believes, is only interested in hearing one thing, and Jessica is not able to decide or to talk about that. The problem between them is the same problem that was there when Jessica was eighteen and won her scholarship. Her mother believes in the garden and in the care of its soil.

The window in Jessica's old bedroom, where she slept every night when she was a bright little girl, is so diminutive it might have been made for a pantry rather than for a bedroom and it is positioned oddly low down on the wall. To see out of the window into the garden Jessica has to lean forward and duck her head. This action makes the shadow across her back heavier. It increases the volume of her form and fills and deepens the picture plane. She leans forward in this way and watches her mother toiling in the garden and her breasts seem darker and heavier and to pull her shoulders down and to round the line of her backbone. After a while Jessica eases her position on the bed, which squeaks. She is resenting her mother for still being out there. It might be that her mother has wilfully survived. That her mother has waited a whole lifetime, her persistence an intentional provocation, a denial of change, holding things up that should have moved on and become wan and distant and mellowed with the passage of time and forgetting. Jessica is prevented, by this lack of change, from experiencing nostalgia for her past. It is a past that has been prevented from becoming mysterious or spiritual for her. It is a past that is still just real.

The weather is warm again and Jessica is wearing a sleeveless blouse in a deep blue cotton. So there is this sudden division of light and dark. The light falling across her bare arm makes it look like an arm cast in some resilient metal, yellow bronze. Her arm, which is towards me, is more suggestive than her features, which are rather lost. Like the room her features don't accept the light but shunt it back against the window, so that there is this obliterating effect, rather than modelling.

In Canberra the following week she talks to me

about her mother again. I'm drawing her and she starts talking, as if her mother is always on her mind. She says, 'When she picks up a handful of that soil and sniffs it the way you saw her doing, she's sniffing herself. That's all a Keal woman's supposed to know. Soil improvement! Improving the soil on that stony little patch of ground. That's all that's ever mattered. It was the point of everything when I was a child. It was all that was ever talked about. The condition of the soil.'

There's impatience and anger and resentment in the way Jessica speaks about this. She apologises and says she must be boring me and promises not to speak of it again. But she can't keep this promise. She's sitting in the studio looking out the window at my almond tree and the neglected orchard and she's got nothing to do but think about these things that are going on in her life.

'I was bending over the bed unpacking,' she says, breaking the silence again. She promises not to go on too long but to just say this one thing. 'It was that first day. I'd just arrived. I was planning on staying with her for a few days. I was bending over the bed unpacking my things and putting them away in the chest of drawers and I glanced out the window with this sudden realisation that she'd still be out there, just as she had been the morning I left, when I went up the hill with my bags to wait for the mailman to take me into town for the last time, and I looked back and she was bending over in the garden. A weed had caught her eye and I had to call out so that she'd look up and see me wave to her for the last time.

'And she *was* there.

'Then I realised she'd always been in my mind. That she'd always been in my mind in this way, waiting for something from me that we'd never talked about. Waiting for me to see something her way. I stood there in my old bedroom for the first time since I was a kid, bent over the bed looking out the window at her, and I had this feeling that she'd waited for me to come home and solve this thing for her and for myself, whatever it was, for thirty years. And I started to see that she'd always been this active, this powerful, presence in my mind and that I'd never really got away from her at all. I nearly repacked everything and left right then. It frightened me. You know what it's like down there, that enormous silence, that continuous crackling and buzzing. There wasn't anyone to talk to about it. I tried writing to Caroline. But writing's never the same as talking. There are some things you can't write. I hadn't thought about any of this. I hadn't expected anything like this when I decided to come back. I thought I'd been pretty clever getting this visiting fellowship in Canberra, close to the valley, where I could quietly organise something. I was going to sort things out for her. I was going to find a nice place for her. Then settle up my affairs and just go back and get on with my life in England.'

In April we got the first touches of frost. I like the cooler weather. I was glad the summer was over and I was feeling more optimistic. I'd done a few promising pieces. The only work I did was on the project with Jessica. For fun I even did a few drawings of Caroline. They were based on slim evidence. Jessica was amused. 'Not a bit like her,' she said. 'I must have given you the wrong impression.'

I'd begun to get together some images that I could sustain a bit of belief in. I painted a Hammershoi, the Dane who painted portraits of women in dun-coloured rooms, reading, their features concealed or with their backs to the viewer. A tonalist. That's what I did with Jessica's mother. The little story she'd given me. A small private vertical oil, seventeen by nine centimetres; the unperturbed figure of her mother in her antique garden, bent over in the steep light, hoeing her earth, the brim of her oily tan fedora concealing her features. The black and gold hills billowing around her as they have always billowed around her at evening. It was through the frame of the window. The puzzle of Jessica's childhood. The dry sound of the hoe, the deepest sound of Jessica's childhood. Something precious offered and withheld. Intensity retreating as she advances towards it. The silence. The unattainable. Something like that. I don't know whether Jessica believed any of this or not. I never mentioned it to her. The story's my secret. How else can you do it?

I'd be tempted to paint with only black and grey if it weren't for the need to sell my pictures. Poor old *Henry* is black and grey, except for the dab of sepia that people stupidly mistake for a pocket handkerchief. *Why is he sitting up?* And of course the mocking yellow slash that's not understood as the daffodils that were in his room that day. Poor old Henry's friends. He was a good doctor who loved life. A low-risk candidate for heart failure. He had a perfect life. A perfect career. One marriage, two children, a boy and a girl, and three grandchildren before he died without getting any warning. A perfect shining life that was a model for everyone's envy. Except you couldn't envy Henry for long. He wouldn't let you. He welcomed you. He shamed you into liking him. He understood your envy and he forgave you and he drew you in to his pleasure and you became part of it. He was modest and utterly brilliant and he knew it and it delighted him and embarrassed him a little. He wasn't sitting up, he was slipping sideways. Plunging! Going over the edge. When they complained about my picture, I should have reminded them that a portrait's always a portrait of the artist. Except that nothing's ever as simple as aphorisms. Whenever we're tempted to try them on, we discover that their general truths never quite fit our particular realities. All the untidy bits are left hanging out, the important bits, the inexplicable stuff that nothing resolves, and we discover again that those explanations don't help because they don't belong to our present reality but belong to something in the language, to that other dimension. The cover-up.

The wisp of silver smoke rises from the log in the wide hearth behind her mother and passes up the chimney through a shaft of sunlight, the kitchen fragrant with the smell of burning redgum and autumn sunshine. And beneath it the smell of earth. Her mother's hands are large and knobbly. Clubbed roots at the ends of her sinewy arms. Bronze and supple as the roots of old roses. They tell us everything about her. Her head is large. Enormous. She's shrinking. She's closing down around her skeleton. The veins coming out into the open. The work of all those years coming out of her at last. It's coming out of conceal-ment. The past eroding out of Jessica's mother as we sit here drinking tea from porcelain cups with roses on them in her smoky kitchen, our little speeches floating about, joyless in the deep silence of the Keal house, a magpie warbling intricately on the verandah, distant and from another time. In the hearth behind Jessica's mother the silver smoke drifts up from the log. And now and then the log creaks, its fibres being eased apart by the greater strength of fire. Talking. Things easing out. And the sound making us look round at the fire.

The ruins of the past eroding out of Enid Keal. It's an antique city poking up out of the desert, elaborate, desiccated, abandoned. Her hands lift the blue teapot, her right hand gripping the handle, her left hand holding the lid so it won't slip off. Dark mottled things, the veins bulging and straining on the surface.

And when she's finished pouring she tucks a wisp of hair behind her ear and lifts her face to me, to look, once, with her crumpled mouth and her apple-pale eyes, into mine. Not curiosity, not inquisitiveness, but a message. She's not interested in having me around their place.

There's no limit to our vanity. We're all impersonating the person we'd like to be like. We're surprised when someone we consider to be extremely ugly or stupid is as vain about their appearance as we are about our appearance. But we shouldn't be. We even want to look good on our deathbed. You can't tell what people are thinking by looking at their faces. The face is a mask of vanity. We practise it all our lives. We're good at it. This is the paradox. It's our art. Concealment. Deception.

After tea Jessica takes me down the track behind the house and shows me the creek. Once we're out of the house she cheers up. The weight goes off her and she lights a cigarette. At the creek she squats down by the edge of the stream and stares at the water running over the stones.

'This is it,' she says with feeling, reaching her hand

out and letting the water run through her fingers. We're under the canopy of the sweeping branches of the casuarinas. The air's cool and fragrant with the water and the trees. We're below the house and the garden. We've crossed a grassy flat with black wattle trees and rabbit holes and blackberries. Jessica takes her shoes off and rolls her jeans up and she steps into the shallow water. She gives a little gasp and grabs my arm to steady herself. But we avoid looking at each other directly. We avoid each other's eyes. We make a point of that. It's a signal that we're not taking anything for granted. That there's nothing to *be* taken for granted. We're letting each other know that we're not asking for anything. So maybe we're asking for everything. It's not easy to tell. She wades out into the stream. Little brown fish dart around her ankles.

She goes right across the creek, dipping the rolled ends of her jeans into the water, and she climbs the bank on the other side. There's a cattle track there. It's where the white-faced cows come down to drink and they've eroded a path. The soft green couch grass grows right up to the edges of the path, as if a gardener in a city garden has arranged the effect to look natural. She reaches up for a branch and hauls herself onto the high bank. She stands there looking off at a view that

I can't see from where I am down here in the bed of the creek. She stands straight, making a picture of herself, then she stretches, embracing her childhood playground. Her bare arms in the sunlight.

She knows I'm watching. She's proud of the way she looks. She's proud of being in good shape, of not having let herself go. She'd like people to think of her as a woman in her prime. She's like someone who is with their biographer. She wants honesty, of a kind. She doesn't want any of the small or the mean things to register with me.

I think she's about to turn round and say something to me, maybe invite me over, but she moves off, going over the bank and out of sight without saying anything. Maybe she'd forgotten I was there. Maybe she assumed I'd occupied myself examining the creek. I sit down in the shade of the casuarinas and I lean against a fallen tree and I wait for her. I could follow, but I don't. I don't feel I've been asked to follow. I don't always only go where I'm invited. I wasn't invited to her reception in the common room. But there it is.

While I wait I get out my little notebook and do some small sketches of her standing up on the bank by the cattle track hauling herself aloft with the branch, her bare arm extended, smooth and pale and strong, this limb reaching out and the rest of her coming along after it, like an afterthought, the arm doing all the work, being all the person, twice its normal size but just exactly right. The slim branch of the casuarina pliable and springy, bending and responding to the strength in her grip. Drawings no bigger than two centimetres square. Later I think I hear her coming back with someone and I stop drawing and listen, surprised that there's someone else here besides us. But it's the water going over the stones, making the sound of people talking.

I wasn't a child prodigy. The idea of being an artist came to me late. I'd always kept up a bit of drawing and watercolour from when I was a kid, but it became a secret thing that I did for myself. It was a private passion that I concealed from the people I worked with. As a labourer and a farm worker I never met anybody who cared about art. I never saw my drawing as something that could have any value for anyone but myself. I still have a couple of those early notebooks. They're filled with my commentary as well as my drawings. Titles that I elaborated into stories. Titles have always been important to me. They've always been half the story. Drawing was my diary, a private listening device for what was going on on the inside. I was twenty before it was suggested to me that I could take myself seriously as an artist. I saw at once that I was being offered freedom – from having to do a job. And I took the offer. People had expected something from me. This had puzzled me. I could never see what it was until this woman, whom Jessica reminded me of, took my drawing seriously for me. She took it for granted that I had a choice. And I believed her. I've invented many reasons since then for why I became an artist and what art means to me, but really it has always been freedom. And whenever I've decided the artist's life was too arduous for me, it's been the prospect of losing my freedom that's driven me back to art.

An artist is free. That's the greatest thing there is about a life of art. At every moment you see your life to the end. You're not working your way towards something. You're not waiting for an event in the future. You're whole. You belong to yourself. Success is the only thing that has threatened this for me. Success made art my profession and my livelihood. Success meant I no longer viewed art as a simple choice, which was the greatest thing about art, the fact that I chose to do it. The choice disconnected me. I became detached. It was a kind of daily suicide that I survived to repeat again the next day. It was the most arrogant thing, the most selfish, and it humbled me. Freedom frightened me. I was afraid each day when I had to decide to begin work again. Nothing affirmed that decision except my own choice. With success I lost the fear of choosing freedom for myself and I lost the best thing in art. It was Jessica who linked me up to that fear in myself again. The intimate image I have of her in this portrait in front of me, an image in which I am content to recognise myself. In my portrait of Jessica, revelation has become an act of concealment. It's a fiction. A private mystery. An entry in my diary in which the identity of the true subject has been hidden.

I didn't fight with my father about becoming an artist. It was never that classic fight between a father and son about doing something useful that drove me away from home when I was a boy. I didn't know I was going to be an artist then and my father couldn't have cared less about money and usefulness. If he had money he gave it away. He shared it. He was careless with his money. He threw it away. They say the Scots are mean but he was recklessly extravagant. At Christmas he'd pick up a dero and bring him home. Was this supposed to be a display of Christian charity? He wasn't a Christian. He always told me and my sister that religion was the great evil and to watch out for it. Which was maybe just a way of having a go at my mother, who'd been raised a Catholic and had taught us to say our prayers. So what was it with him then? His old men at Christmas? He'd sit them up close to the coal fire, which he'd stoke with a bucket of wet dross, in his own chair in our parlour and they'd start steaming and smelling the place out and he'd give them a glass of neat whisky, which was how he drank it himself then. They'd want to get out. They'd be missing their pals. They didn't feel right sitting in our parlour drinking and eating and having a good time. It wasn't a good time for them. But he'd insist. He wouldn't let them get away. With me and my sister watching them they were ashamed of themselves. And we were expected to be respectful to them. They were his long-lost brothers. He was telling himself a fairy story. He flattered them. 'Here's one of the few men in England you can trust,' he'd tell us, putting his arm round the old codger's shoulders and making us come up and shake him by the hand. He was rescuing *himself* from ruin. He'd forget about being generous to us. The dero would get all his attention. And after a few whiskies he'd take the old fellow up to the Baring Arms and that's the last we'd see of our father for Christmas. We were glad and we were sorry to see the back of him. His old men at Christmas and later his broken-backed books. They were his freedom. I learned to despise the meanness of his vision before I realised this. By then it was too late. We were never reconciled.

I didn't do any formal training. I never went to art school. I only do portraits. People. Us. You don't find me doing those enormous urban landscapes. I don't know how to do that kind of architectural stuff, or motor cars and kitchen appliances, or those surrealist ideas where one thing's becoming something else. Metaphors in paint. I can't stand all that banality. All that symbolism, it's too literal. It doesn't interest me. It doesn't deal with the facts of my condition. I'm limited. I admit that. My lack of training has always limited my choices and my tastes. And maybe that's made it easier for me.

I never hesitated. I wasn't distracted by other possibilities. I didn't consider anything else. It was us from the word go. Portraits. It was never another subject. It was me. Myself. The solitary act of painting reconnecting me to something begun in childhood and not completed. When I can't work there's nothing. It's all futile. There's not a sufficient reason for living. It's always been the mask. And I soon realised it was just glimpses. Bits and pieces. Fragments. There was no way out of that. The more open I was the deeper I was hiding something.

That day by the creek Jessica gave me a private picture of herself. It was a picture of a woman sitting in a comfortable armchair looking out of a window onto a summer landscape. I kept the idea without consciously considering it. It stayed with me. It was simple and there was something optimistic in it. She said it was a picture of herself she'd always had in her mind. She couldn't remember when she'd got it. In this picture she has her back to the viewer. She's facing the view (it's another Hammershoi). Well, naturally things got changed, but I kept the idea of her looking out of a window. We're always looking out of windows. They're not just there to let the light in. If there's a window, sooner or later we look out of it. We like to look in windows too. But that's not so easy. Into the private goings on of our neighbours. So there was nothing remarkable about her private picture of herself sitting in a chair gazing out these ample windows onto a beautiful summer day. It was just this little private view of herself. And that's what attracted me to it. A commonplace thing.

She was gone for more than an hour. She didn't come back the way she'd gone, across the creek where the cattle had broken down the bank and made a track, but came up quietly behind me. A stone clicked and I turned round and she was standing there looking down at me. She was laughing at something. To herself. The light was shining up from the water into her eyes. It was an effect I'd noticed before in someone else, I couldn't remember when. She was lit up with her exercise and with some excitement of her thoughts and with the way she had surprised me.

I closed my notebook and put it in my pocket. She sat next to me on the stones and said, in a bantering tone, 'You're not going to let me see, I suppose?'

I took out my notebook and gave it to her. She examined the little drawings with intense interest. And that's when she said she'd always had this picture of herself, just telling it to me, of herself sitting by these ample windows looking out at the sunny day. She was touching the drawings with the tips of her fingers, as if she expected to experience texture. There was a movement of the air and I smelt the water on her.

'Have you been for a swim?' I asked, watching her swimming naked in the sunlit creek under the canopy of the casuarinas.

She flourished the notebook. 'It was our bath,' she said. 'Just down there. There's a deep hole at the bend of the creek. I went to see if it was still there. The creek changes. I used to bathe with my grandmother every day. Even when it was cold and raining we'd come down and have our bath. The water was so cold after a frost we'd scream.'

She tells me this as if she's not just remembering herself as a girl but is still that girl now, as if she's just been out there in the landscape becoming that girl again, going to this swimming hole in a way I'm not going to be able to understand, then coming back and sneaking up on me just to see if she could be that quiet in the bush, doing the kind of thing you do when you're still young. But the way she has of talking like this keeps a little barrier up between us, her manner remarking on the barrier, reminding me it's there, as if she's saying there's no way I'm going to get her portrait right. She hands my notebook back to me.

And she says, 'They look like drawings for a sculpture. Little bronze images. Detached. The sort of thing you imagine Rodin doing, putting everything into one arm. As if the arm can be the whole person.' She's looking over my shoulder at the notebook that I'm looking at. Then she looks directly at me. And her gaze is candid and open and curious as she's searching my features. Asking herself a question. I'm reminded of our meeting in the corridor at the university the evening I was feeling low and exhausted and wasn't taking any notice of things around me. Suddenly it's her again, that woman for an instant, fleetingly, looking into me, expecting something from me, offering me something of herself. Then she reaches forward and picks up a stone and the moment has passed.

I put the notebook back in my pocket.

It's a touchy business for everyone this. She's not sure what it's leading to. I'm annoyed by her reference to Rodin. She's right, of course, but she needn't have said it. Artists hate people to remind them of where they're drawing their ideas from. She might have guessed *that*. You have to start somewhere. I'm thinking, she didn't pick Hammershoi. She only picks the ones everyone knows. You can't reinvent the whole thing every time you paint a picture. It's what the writer Nabokov called 'lawful property in the free city of the mind'.

I look at her and wait for her to notice that I'm looking at her with all this in my mind. I say, 'I could smell the water on you when you got back, Jessica.'

She shuffles at the stones with her bare toes. Maybe she's shy about the image in my mind of herself naked, swimming in the private bath as a young girl with her grandmother, or on her own in the autumn sunlight today, no longer a young girl. Maybe that's it. Maybe it's not an image she wants me to have.

'The Araluen creek,' she says. 'There's something about the water. The old people used to talk about it. They wouldn't drink the water below the junction with the river.'

We watch the special water of the Araluen creek flowing past just beyond our feet. An abundant stream as clear as glass. The notebook in my shirt pocket is pressing heavily against my chest. And there's that shrieking in the air, rising and falling and sidling along the creek in waves, searching the wavelengths, tuning to something, a succession of tones searching for a certain resolution, elaborating the silence of this place. Birds call high in the forest, cries of alarm echoing among the gullies and the zamia palms, back and forth among the antique cycads. And we're waiting.

I'm expecting her to say something about herself, or maybe about her mother. I can feel her thinking. I'm remembering a painting which my wife bought for me in London more than twenty years ago. It's a Sickert. A Mornington Crescent nude, *contre jour*. It hangs in my bedroom in my house in Canberra opposite *Henry*, arrested in his sideways plunge. In the Sickert the dark form of the naked woman shimmers against the light. The blaze of light along the edge of the naked female body, that was Sickert's contribution. The woman's body is heavy and flowing and is in the splendid assurance of middle-age. She is raised on her elbow, anticipating the attention of the viewer. We're always seduced into reading the world as waiting for our thoughts to be completed.

Jessica lobs a stone into the creek. It's an impatient gesture and punctuates the sense of strain and unease and maybe even disappointment that's growing up between us. I'm disappointed in myself. She sorts aggressively through the stones between her legs, rattling them against each other and she selects another and throws it, this time hard, right across the creek and onto the far bank, as if she's testing how far she can throw, testing her strength. The stone hits the bank with a thud.

'I was married once,' she says. And she runs her palm over the water-worn stones, back and forth, rattling them against each other, something in her mood that she wishes to pass off as playful and teasing, but which is more akin to resentment. 'There aren't any flat stones in the Araluen,' she says, and she breathes and looks at me. Something of that challenge and enmity in her gaze. And then she tells me this story about how she came to get married. And while she's telling me she's selecting stones and tossing them into the creek. We watch the stones lobbing into the water. She's keeping our attention off herself with this. Keeping the situation fluid. Not letting things lock up.

'We were friends,' she says. 'It was a good friendship. We lived together for two years. We took our holidays together. One day a group of us were going to Austria. We were going skiing. The night before we were due to leave on the skiing holiday we met at a restaurant in Soho and we all got drunk. Someone made the observation that he and I were the only ones in the group who weren't married. So we decided to get married and join our friends later, so that we could all be on the holiday as a group of married couples. After the ceremony we stayed at a hotel in the West End and tried to behave the way we thought a newly married couple would behave. We both loathed it but we persisted with the pretence of it. We could feel it doing us harm but we didn't quit. We didn't mention the harm to each other. We didn't say we weren't enjoying it. We pretended we were enjoying ourselves. It was as if the whole thing was a test of our nerve, to see who would give in first. But neither of us gave in. We didn't know how to be truthful about it without feeling we'd failed. You know when you cut your finger, or you do yourself some sort of injury, and you're aware the second before you do it that you're going to do it and yet you don't stop yourself from doing it. A kind of will beyond your own will takes over and you just go on with it and you harm yourself, and then the pain is a relief and a punishment. You've satisfied some awful inner prompting, some grim and childish impulse has been satisfied. And you realise this thing is underneath your normal life and it can surface at any time and harm you. You've hurt yourself on purpose. And now you're satisfied, but you're ashamed of yourself. You've done it out of spite. For no reason. *I'm not going to be your friend any more*, that kind of thing, that little girls say to each other to be as hurtful as they possibly can be when they're trying to control everyone. I'm sure people kill themselves, or even kill other people, while they're in the grip of this.' She threw another stone and we watched it strike the water. 'I felt capable of killing him. Of course we didn't go skiing. There are still times when I feel cheated out of that holiday. We couldn't stand each other after that. We couldn't stand the sight of each other. It was over. We'd admitted we'd never really known anything about each other before, despite our friendship and those years of living together. We never discussed it. I still run into him from time to time. At conferences and that sort of thing. I think he's happy. He's a grandfather.'

Jessica held another stone, ready to lob it into the Araluen creek. 'I don't know what made me think of all this,' she said, a little sad. She was silent for a long time. Then she came out with this, 'It's coming back to Australia, coming back here, to my mother's, to the garden and everything. It's punishing myself. I've always kept away. I love this place. That's why I've always kept away from it. I hated this place when

I was eighteen. I couldn't wait to escape. And when I came down the road last year and saw that old post-and-rail fence falling down I cried. I sat in the car and cried. My gran split the timber for that fence when I was a kid. I sat up there under the walnut tree watching her driving the wedges. We used to call it the new fence. My mother probably still refers to it as the new fence. My mother never had anything to say. She just waited for me to clear out. She knew I would. Now she thinks I've come back. She thinks I've finished with whatever it was I had to go away for. She expects me to start fixing the fences and putting things back in order again, like they were when she was a kid. She doesn't say anything. She's never said anything. But I know that's what she's thinking.'

Jessica lobbed the stone. 'Come on,' she said. 'I'll show you the rest of the place. We can walk round it in five minutes.'

But we didn't get up. I'd been drawing while she was talking. She looked over my shoulder at what I'd done. We stayed there till it got dark.

I began a series of nude studies in oil late that night when I got home, working from my drawings of the figure up on the bank. My studio was beginning to fill up with images of her. It wasn't the look in her eyes that interested me with these little oil sketches. If she'd decided to stay in the valley when she was a girl, instead of rushing off to London like everyone else was doing in those days, she would have had the physique to manage the garden. She would have had the build for it. Her mother was right. I saw Jessica lifting a redgum fencepost, embracing it against her body and dropping it into the hole. I see her raising the bar and ramming the clay and the stones until they're so tight the post hums when the bar strikes the ground at its base. Her arms have kept their strength. And her thighs, on which she pivots against the swing of her torso when she's doing something physical and is absorbed in the action of it. So these pictures are of Jessica labouring. They're notes. They absorb me for weeks. I don't stretch the canvases but pin them up on the wall opposite the windows, a row of them, a dozen side by side and I work on them all at the same time, going from one to another, building them up, memory and guesswork mostly, and those little drawings I did that day down by the Araluen creek behind her mother's place.

My father resented having all his time taken up looking after the two of us. My sister and me. Having to work for money to keep us all going. He never got over that. He thought he should have had a chance to do something himself after the war and that we took it away from him. And he was right. It was true. He was cheated. We weren't the whole story, of course, but our existence was another thing to add to the list. We cheated him. He had once expected to achieve something, then we denied him the time and the peace of mind. So he took his revenge on us. I accused him once. I told him straight out, it made my heart stop to do it, 'You've got no dignity Dad.' He just cursed me. People who have nothing turn on each other. You see them staggering about screaming at each other. They hate doing it. Their lives are filled with remorse because of it. But they can't help it. They just go on doing it. It takes over and makes them wretched. It's like they were listening to someone else screaming and yelling. It's not really them. They know that. They're not really like that. They can't explain to anyone why they do it.

We don't hesitate now. We blame him for everything. He's the one we blame so we don't have to blame ourselves. So we don't have to be self-critical. He was the polar bear in the zoo, pacing backwards and forwards in his pit. We hung over the railing and tormented him. We didn't have to do anything. Just being there looking at him was enough to drive him mad. If we let him out we'd be the first ones he'd kill. We were fascinated. We used to get too close sometimes. We used to dare each other to get close. We loved him. He got hold of her one day, my sister, and threw her against the wall. He terrified us. He terrified himself. More than sixty years later I can still feel her little body hitting the wall. 'Here he comes, quick!' We screamed and grabbed hold of each other. It used to make our flesh crawl with fear, the sound of him coming up the stairs of the flats. We'd go quiet. We'd try not to be doing anything. We'd try not to be there. We were always hoping he'd be in a good mood. He knew he was supposed to be everything and he knew he was nothing. And all he saw when he looked up was us hanging over the edge of his pit tormenting him.

They were all like that in our neighbourhood. Everyone's father was like that in those days. We were afraid of them. We don't have to ask ourselves why. The bit of promise they'd had, the hope, it was embittered. They went around in a rage. Even on a good day the rage was only just below the surface. Even on a happy day you knew the murderous impulses were only just being held in check. The balloon could go up any second. You waited for it. You watched your step. Any little thing could trigger it. You knew you were going to make a mistake sooner or later. You waited for it. You were accident prone.

They never had a chance.

Once when he came home on leave from France we devised a play. A little drama of our own to help everyone forget the big drama that was going on over there. We were staying with our mother in this beautiful old house in the country. He never touched her. I never saw him hit my mother, or even threaten to hit her. The Malt House, it was called. Pink tea roses grew up the walls, and when you looked out the windows of the attic there they were, framing your face.

My sister and I hung out the window with our arms round each other's necks and our hot cheeks pressed together, and my mother went down on the lawn and took a snapshot of us. That's us! An oval vignette by Antoine Watteau. We ran around half

94

naked in the heat that summer doing what we liked. It was our billet. We were on the move in those days. They got us out of London to avoid the bombs. He never knew where we'd be when he got his next leave. It was an adventure. The woman who owned the Malt House encouraged us to have some fun. There's another snapshot of me and my sister in our drawers trying to uproot a fruit tree, with the woman standing there laughing at us and egging us on. We're tiny pale things with hardly any flesh on us. Our ribs stick out and we look eager and excited and old. Our eyes are black dots. Baby bears in the zoo, practising for the real thing. I was surprised by the tenacity of that tree. Our combined strength had no effect. I learned something about trees. About the world.

We performed the play in the attic, which was our living room while we were at the Malt House. The attic was a sunny room with three dormer windows that looked out over a view of green fields towards tight dark woods and some smoky hills. I don't remember which one of us was the author of the play. I was supposed to protect my sister from the witch. I was nervous. I knew the task was beyond me. My mother was the witch. But when my mother made her entrance, draped in a black silk shawl and shaking a yard broom at us, instead of saying, Go away you big black witch! I panicked and screamed, 'Go away you big black bitch!'

We rolled on the floor laughing till we felt sick. And every time it came to that line in the play we fell about laughing and could never get to the end of the scene. We didn't complete the play. I don't remember what was supposed to happen in the end. We stuck on the word bitch and it stayed with us for ever. It's still with us. It's as far as we got in my family. We never got to the end of the story.

In the portrait I did of my agent, Michael Vay, with his back to the viewer in his gallery, he's looking at a portrait of me facing the viewer. Which was just a picture of a man in a dark blue suit with his back to us looking at a portrait. But everyone recognised Michael. No one doubted it was him, Michael Vay, the director of v, the dealer everyone wants to be with. 'It's him,' they said and they had a good laugh. No one commented on the absence of his likeness. What does resemblance consist of? The absence of his facial features, that is. Which proved to be superfluous to the portrait. And *he* liked it! I'd sent him up. I'd told the truth about him. And he liked that. He bought it from me. It's hanging in his dining room. 'I'll never sell it.' This is what he says. But that's a lie. With Michael everything's for sale. That's what Michael's like. It's the way he sees things. He's not like me. I need this place. I need to own it. I'm not going to sell it. I'd be lost without it. Michael surrounds himself with possessions but he doesn't need to own any of them. I need to own the few little things I keep around me. They're not much by Michael's standards but all the same I don't want to part with them. They're not for sale. Michael couldn't care less. One thing's as good as another to him. He'll sell one thing and go and buy something else. There's always something new whenever you see him. He's really not acquisitive, it's me who's acquisitive. He just needs to make money. That's what keeps him happy. Making a profit on things. It's where his joy in life comes from. It doesn't take much to make Michael happy.

But there's more to him than that. He loves artists. Showing people my portrait of him makes Michael happy. He wants all his important visitors to see it. The clients. The aficionados. The collectors. It's a phase with him. It's the first thing he wants them to see when they get to his house. 'Come and see this!' he says, and he drags them through the place before they've had a chance to say anything about anything. Before he's given them a drink. And we pull up in the dining room and there it is. It's huge. A little man with a bald head in a blue suit facing a wall with a large portrait of me on it. 'That's what the bastard thinks of me,' he says. And he laughs and grabs me round the shoulders and hugs me as if he's my brother, or my father. 'You bastard!' he says, dragging me around so they'll all think we're in love.

It's an aside. A slice of life. My life. The way it was then. That's all it is. The side of my life I told Jessica I'd like to do without. 'If I had the strength,' I said to her, meaning if I had the moral strength, 'I'd do without all that stuff. I'd clean up my act. I'd be more ascetic, I'd be sharper, I'd be leaner and meaner. I wouldn't bother going to Sydney.' And she said that was silly and that I ought to just determine my own life and not worry about those things.

She doesn't understand. The artist's freedom is double edged. If an artist keeps to himself that's it, nothing happens. You've got to get out and meet the right people. You've got to be a bit of a showman, a performer. You've got to succeed in other ways than with your art. Pictures aren't enough on their own. Otherwise you're Charles Despiau and no one knows how good you are and you don't get any commissions till you're fifty. It's easy for her to say that. But I'm not that strong. That's Bonnard. He was strong enough for that. He never faltered. You only have to look at Brassaï's photograph of him. Pierre Bonnard, the Frenchman. There's a portrait without vanity! Just a bit of one cheek and a touch of moustache sticking out from under his hat. It's only a fragment. But it's enough.

My father was right. 'Be a man, son!' That's the last thing he called out to me on Paddington railway station when he was waving goodbye. I looked round at the sound of his voice and saw him wave. I still see him waving now. I can still feel his despair. His defeated hope. God knows what he meant. I thought he meant be cruel, be hard, show no feeling for anything and stand up to all kinds of pain and disappointment without complaint. I never even tried. I knew I couldn't do that. And if Michael Vay ever stopped treating me like a precious son I'd be sick with worry. Michael enjoys being effaced by me. Michael earned my view of him. It proved his necessity and revealed my weakness. My weakness for success and money and for having aficionados celebrating my work while I enjoyed the luxury of pretending none of it mattered to me. Who wants the tragic life of Charles Despiau? It's our conspiracy. Me and Michael. He looks at the world through me. He's a dealer and he deals with the world for me. We still allow each other the freedom to play this game, so we can each keep a little private space open for the real thing. And maybe I do love him, in a way. A word is never going to decide these things. Words are powerless to decide these things. Words don't touch the emotions. Words are part of the mask. We know there's always someone listening for an echo of themselves in everything we say. There's always someone reading our thoughts over our shoulder as we write them down, or watching us paint our little images and commenting on the way we're doing it, criticising us, deriding our weaknesses and our lack of courage, and urging us to try something new and more challenging. It's me listening for Jessica's private thoughts and imagining I hear them, and it's Jessica knowing she's being listened to. There's always someone out there ready to tell you how you should be doing it.

Art is more interesting than reality. Art is more interesting than life. But it's only glimpses and guesswork. With art you're never going to get the whole picture. There's a blankness at the heart of each of us.

Art is our dispute with that blankness, that mute place. Art is our dispute with reality. You have to find the emotional drive, the engine of necessity, like Bonnard, if you're going to keep going with new projects and not give up and start repeating yourself. It always begins with a question. A doubt. And then you're off, in search of yourself, and it's not long before you come across these strange tracks and you ask what kind of creature would have made tracks like these. And you go in search of this elusive creature. And they're your own tracks. And that's what you have to learn. And every time you learn it you're learning it for the first time. You surprise yourself.

We're in my studio and I'm showing Jessica the little oil of her mother. It's late. We're both tired but we're happy. We're in that tired, happy, satisfied state you sometimes get to when you've done a good day's work. We've had a long session. She's talked a lot and I've painted a lot. We've been dealing with things and we've got this sense between us of companionship and respect. And it's more than that too, but what can you say? Like I said, it's only glimpses. That's all you can ever get. Guesses. Small things. She's surprised I've painted a picture of her mother. I tell her it's not the only picture of her mother I've painted. We're not looking at the perfect image. We're standing here beside each other looking at this picture of her mother, where I've propped it on the solander, and she suddenly takes hold of my hand. And here we are if someone walks in on us, standing side by side in the twilight holding hands.

My sister's older than me. Two years older. And she's taller than me. She's ungainly, angular, gangly, ugly. She always was. Right through school. Her nose is enormous. Her big feet sit out at a silly angle from her bony legs. She's got great knobbly knees that are grey and scarred. She's wearing a school dress. It's a check cotton dress and it's dirty and ripped. I'm face down on the floor and she's sitting on me. I love her and I wish for her sake that she were beautiful. She beats me with her fists, systematically, driving her fists into my back as hard as she can, with all her strength, without fear of reprisal, hurting me. She's going at it. She's doing a real job of work on me. And I'm bearing the beating without complaint. There's a reason for this, only neither of us knows what the reason is. We just know there's a reason. That's what we have in common, this silent knowledge. And my lack of a reaction to her blows enrages her. Beating me hurts her more than it hurts me. Neither of us knows why she beats me. And eventually she begins to cry. 'That was lovely,' I say. 'Don't stop! Keep going!'

She weeps helplessly, pressing into my back with the flats of her hands, kneading the hurting muscles of my back, sobbing without restraint. 'What's up?' I say, as if I'm surprised at her distress, as if this isn't our familiar ritual. As if we're doing it for the first time. She gets off me and she runs in to her room and she slams the door. I follow her and listen at the keyhole. That's what I do. I gaze into space and witness her crying in her room, sitting on her bed staring out of her window, her face wet and streaked with dirt, staring out at the elm trees along the road and the flats opposite. This little girl in her room sitting on her bed crying. My back's hurting. It serves me right. The pain from the beating is severe. I can hardly bear it without groaning. My back will be covered in bruises in the morning. I feel strangely peaceful. Cleaned out. Emptied. I'm at home. I feel like laughing and crying at the same time. I lean down, listening at my sister's bedroom door and I whisper her name, to myself, not loud enough for her to hear. I like to hear her name. Later, after she leaves home, she will abandon the name my mother and father had her christened with and will adopt a strange new name that has been unknown to our family till then. I'll never be able to think of her new name as being her. She'll always be the old name for me. The new name will be a betrayal. It will be as if she has ceased to exist for me when she changes her name. As if she has wanted to cut out that childhood period of her life and me with it. As if she has decided to forget those beatings and the silent knowledge we shared. As if she has had to forget our childhood together and to go on alone. I didn't write to her, ever. Not one letter in all those years. There were times when I would have liked to have written to her, and at those times I probably composed letters to her in my mind. She wrote to me when I had my show in London. But I didn't reply. She wrote to tell me she'd taken a couple of days off her job and had travelled down from Leeds especially to see my show. And I'd been there in the gallery and hadn't recognised her. She'd seen me talking to people and she'd hung about but had thought it best not to interrupt me. *In the end I had to write and tell you*, she wrote. I didn't reply to her letter. I didn't know how. I couldn't start. I couldn't bring myself to address her as her new name. By then for her an old name, but still her new name for me. And I couldn't bring myself to insult her by addressing her as her old name. Our old name for her. My sister. So in the end I let it go. Then eventually so much time had gone by that there was no longer any point in replying. A letter from me after all that time wouldn't have been simply a reply, it would have been an invitation to resume an elaborate contact that had lapsed twenty years ago. I'm not sentimental enough for that.

A while later, two or three years later, I got the news of her death. She had two boys. One of them, the oldest, wrote to me. *Mum often spoke about you to us. I'm only sorry we never had the chance to meet you. You must have been great mates together during the war. She was ill for three years off and on. She had two operations. It was breast cancer.* And so on. I put the letter aside and went on with my work. I was working on an oil study for the *Tan Family*. I was working up to the big one. I was working from notes and information spread all over the studio. I was well into it. I put the letter from my sister's son to one side on my painting trolley and went on applying paint to the canvas. It was as if my sister had crept up quietly while I was working and had closed a door, trying not to disturb me, trying not to interrupt my work with her bit of news, trying not to draw attention to herself, to her death, not wanting to waste my time. The catch on the closing door just making that last click that gives the game away. I could see her creeping away cursing herself for her carelessness in distracting me from my important work.

By lunchtime I realised I hadn't been thinking about the *Tan Family* but had been laying the paint on all morning as if someone else was doing it for me. I'd been talking to my sister and watching someone else do the painting. The *Tan Family* surprised me. I couldn't believe what I'd done. I knew I'd done something good. But I hadn't been aware of painting it. I'd been acknowledging my sister in the gallery ·in Mayfair. We were laughing and embracing and saying what a great thing it was and who would have thought when we were kids in the flats that we'd be doing this one day. And there was her husband and her two boys – whom I'd never had the grace or the generosity to meet in real life – and I was taking them all to dinner at the Savoy. I could still feel her little body hitting that wall. Trembling afterwards. Taking the blame for something I'd done, I'll bet.

I set up my easel and the rest of my gear in the open passage outside her bedroom door and that's where I began to paint my first study. She called to me from inside the room, half-joking, in the half-light, the room resisting the light in that way that was to interest me. 'How do you want me?' she called.

'On the bed,' I said, half-joking.

'Like this?' she suggested. And suddenly we were children playing a game together. I looked in to see what she was doing. She was sitting on the side of the bed in half-profile, the light dancing along the edges of her. The short sleeve of her blouse and her arm again, pale and luminous and pushing itself towards me, turned at the shoulder. She was exaggerating herself. Posing.

'Yes,' I said. 'You look great. You look really great.' She did. She looked like the kind of woman every woman hopes to become. Herself.

But she wasn't in it. That first study was of her absence. That's what it turned out to be. The room through the door seen from the passage. Vertical, enclosed, dark. The door frame an additional frame within the simple composition. Cramping the perspective. Forcing the viewer to look more searchingly, more inwardly, into the narrow vertical enclosure. The bed a short section of horizontality, stopped, blocked at either end, pushed up and curtailed tightly. I kept her right out of it.

I didn't mean to.

I was painting something else. But you never know what you're doing till you've done it. Till you've challenged the first offer.

'You paint the figure in afterwards?' she asked, coming round to see what I'd done, pleased to be surprised by this novel idea. Ready for anything.

'No,' I said. 'That's it.'

I was packing up. I went on packing up. She just stood there looking at it. She didn't say a word. The lack of a figure where she'd been prepared for the first image of herself in oil, sitting there posed on the bed all morning. 'It's not the portrait,' I said, falling into the trap of explaining myself. 'I can't do you yet. I don't know what to do. I don't know what I'm doing. You seem to think I'm planning things. I'm not. I'm just trying things out. I'm putting things down so I can erase them. I'm still at that stage.'

I sounded impatient. I *was* impatient. I was unsure of myself, so I didn't tell her I was pleased with the picture. I was accustomed to painting the portraits of

108

strangers. This was different. 'I wouldn't have a bloody clue, Jessica,' I said. 'It may not work. I'm not unhappy with this. It looks okay to me.' Which I suppose she hears as *take it or leave it*.

We stood there in the passage outside her old bedroom looking at the picture. I could hear her mother in the kitchen, poking and scraping in the hearth. 'I've done something. It's a start. That's all.'

Outside she smoked a cigarette and watched me while I packed up. *Why did you let me sit there all day thinking you were doing my portrait? You could have said. You could have said something. I feel such an idiot.* That's what she was thinking. I could feel her thinking it. Her silence was a test of character which she was imposing on herself. I'd rather she'd have come straight out with it.

'I'm doing your portrait, Jessica. Okay?' I said. 'It's how I work.' My back was aching. I needed to sit down and lean against something hard. In the studio I sit on the floor when it gets too much and press my back into the solander. I press my back hard into the brass drawer handles of the solander and that eases the pain.

'There's something in you being there when I

painted it,' I said. 'I can't explain and I'm not going to try,' I said, trying to explain. 'Can I have a drink? Did we bring some wine this time? Where did we put the bag with the wine in it?'

I carried my stuff out to the car and put it in the boot. I laid the wet painting on top. She was in it. For me she was in it. I was in pain. I was angry. I was disappointed. We paint landscapes from our sense of loss and alienation from the real landscape. We paint portraits from our alienation from people. It's nostalgia for company we don't have and can't have. Absence and loss. People we've lost. We're haunted by our memories of them, of ourselves with them. We're always dealing with these things. How to deal with them, that's always the problem. How to visualise them in their absence. We never know what we're doing. Anything heavy-handed defeats it. I know I've missed it if I do what I've been expecting to do. I don't hesitate to destroy that stuff. I distrust it. I'd rather do nothing than understand what I'm doing while I'm doing it.

She was trying to get through it without being difficult. But I hated feeling all that puzzlement and anger from her at this stage. I wanted her to say something. I wanted us to get our anger out and have a good row. But she held on. Not a word. We were both tired.

I said to her, 'You're like your mother you know.' I meant holding on and being silent. But she just thought I was being conventional. I let it go. My back was hurting. I had to sit down.

She looked into the boot of the car at the picture. I was down on the grass, sitting with my back pushed hard against the rear wheel. I closed my eyes and concentrated on the cold hub pressing into the muscles of my back, the pain gradually losing its urgency, spreading out and thinning down to a sensation that was almost pleasant, a background wash.

'If you want to give it away,' I said, 'I don't mind. We can stop now and there's no harm done.'

When there was no reply I opened my eyes. She was half-way up the hill. She was carrying a bottle of wine and a couple of glasses. I watched her. This was her country. She was walking up the hill towards the walnut tree. The sun on her back. I hadn't known I was going to leave her out of the picture till I'd finished it. All along I intended to put her in. But I didn't know how to start painting her. I couldn't find a way of beginning. Every time I made a mark it killed what I was doing with the rest of the picture.

So I kept putting the problem off. Then in the end I began to like the fact of her absence in the picture. Looking at her sitting there on her bed I could feel her absence growing in the painting. Then I realised that's what I was painting. Her absence. That's what this picture was about. It wasn't just a bedroom, it was the absence of Jessica Keal in her own childhood bedroom. It didn't matter if no one else could see that. I could see it.

I got up and opened the boot and looked at the picture again. There was the sense of someone there you can't see, like the window you can't see, where the light's coming from, or being resisted. But it's there. No one doubts that. Like Michael's facial features are there and the expression in his gaze, even though he's got his back to you. They haven't been dealt with literally but they're there all the same. It's a way of putting it to have the subject of the portrait with their back to the viewer. Having them absent is just one step further along that track. What would the judges of the Archibald think of this? Portrait without figure. Jessica Keal withheld. They'd think I was having a lend of them. They'd think I was trying to insult them. I would be. They're touchy about their dignity. For good reason. So they're always on the look-out for smart-arse tactics from the painters. But this is a private thing for me. I know it's not the final job. It's a private study. A preparation. I never thought it would be the end. It never occurred to me to think I was working on the final portrait. How many times did Velasquez paint the portrait of Pope Innocent X? Six? Seven? A dozen times? Did he tell anyone how many goes he had at it? Which one are we talking about when we say Velasquez's portrait of Innocent X? They're all over the place. In Rome. In the Prado. Everywhere. Did he paint one with no one on that throne? We'd still know it was Innocent X. The absence of Innocent X! We'd know that throne anywhere. We think we know everything but it's hindsight. We know exactly what happened, but it's all in reverse order. We think we can reach the truth of events by unravelling them backwards. But the first event was done in the absence of the events that were to follow it. It was done in the absence of foresight. Putting something down in order to erase it. It's dealing with absence. It's an isolated event. The blankness at the heart of the work of art. That's what we lose with our obsession with cause and effect. With the logical order of beginning, middle and end. The absence and the isolation of things. We forget that. The silence that surrounds everything we do while we're doing it. Always. The silence we work in. At the centre. Working with the absence. Our anxiety. Trying to bring something into being there. Hoping to coax it out. Holding our breath. Waiting for that first little sign of presence. That offer. The first shuffling movement in the dark. Through the screen. What's in there? What are we looking at? And then the happy accident, the distraction of our thoughts, the way the paint begins to go on while we're thinking of something else, and suddenly it's happening. It's not our intention. But here it comes. We're alone. We're in the great isolation. Alone with the great absence. It's always the same. With the mute nothing. Just that faint shuffling in our ears. The rushing of our blood. Then it's greeting us. And we've never seen it before. It's the same old thing and we've never seen it before. It's new. It's completely new and unexpected and we know it and we've always known it. It's the trace of ourselves. Look at that! Nothing makes you feel better. It's a drug. It goes through you like a dose of amphetamines and suddenly you're light-headed and light-hearted. You're happy. Just for a little while you've surprised yourself and you're tired but happy.

She was sitting up there in the shade under the walnut tree. I went up the hill after her. I was going to explain to her why she was absent in my picture. I walked up the hill with the explanation ready in my mind. My explanation was going to link us up. I wanted her to see the process the way I saw it. But when I got to the tree I didn't say anything about it. I sat on the ground beside the mound of her grandmother's grave and she handed me a glass of wine and started telling me about the walnut tree and how it had given them this wonderful crop of nuts every year.

'Our cash crop,' she says, looking up into the branches of the tree. 'It never failed. And it's still going. And when it dies the timber will be worth a little fortune.'

We sit there in the shade of the big tree, and when she's finished telling me about it we look down the hill at her mother hoeing in the garden. And we drink the wine. The Keal place laid out below us. Her place. This little clearing here by the creek flat. A chance survival. Rustic. Enchanting. Picturesque. All that. And I know I've got something. I'm not thinking about the Keal place, I'm working along at the painting in my mind. I'm doing the project of her

115

portait and it hardly needs her. I can't do without her, but she's not the main thing. I'm the main thing. Recovering myself. I can never explain this link to her. I'm scared she's going to tell me she's pulling out of it. Maybe she heard my offer after all. She'll say she's run out of time. She won't say she's run out of patience. She'll say it's the pressure of work. We drink the wine and sit there looking down the hill at her mother's place and I wait for her to say something. I can feel it coming.

'When I left for England,' she says, 'the night before I left. We came up here, me and my gran, and she gave me a little bag of nuts from this tree and asked me if I'd take them to our relatives in Devon. That's where this tree came from. My great grandmother brought it out with her. It was a seed-ling. She had it growing in a potato on the voyage out. So I promised Gran I'd take the nuts back but I never did. They're still in a drawer somewhere at home. In my desk, I think. I haven't seen them for years. But I've never chucked them out.'

She says this then she's silent.

'I meant to take them back. I just never did. I've often been in Devon. It used to make me feel guilty thinking of those nuts in the drawer at home.'

'You could still do it,' I say. 'You could still take them back.'

'It's too late. I always resisted making the connection. Between us and them. Here and England. I never made the connection. I still haven't. Mum expects me to stay and look after the garden when she's gone. She thinks that's why I've come home.' She's silent for a bit then she turns to me. 'Everyone's got something like that in their family.' She watches me for a bit. 'It's our refusal to connect things up, isn't it?'

'I can hardly remember anything about my childhood.' I look at her. 'D'you want to go for a swim?' She doesn't reply. I've said this very quickly. Without thinking. Getting away from the subject of my family. I think she's not going to reply.

Then she says, 'I'll show you the swimming hole where Gran and I used to have our bath.' We finish the wine and she props the bottle in the fork of the tree. There's a shimmering in the light now with the wine and the air. There are the grave mounds of her grandmother and her great-grandmother. The Keal women. It's all coming to an end here. All that. We walk down the hill together, the last of the sun in our eyes dazzling us, and there's the click and scrape

117

of her mother's hoe. Our shoulders bump a couple of times, our arms touching, her cool bare arm against mine. The wine has made me a bit breathless. We're unsteady. I say, 'Christ, listen to those bloody insects,' and she laughs and we let our arms touch again. We're tense and self-conscious and alert and clumsy with each other now.

She's gone. Back to England. Just for the break, she said. But I had the feeling even then she wouldn't be coming back. I promised her I'd go down to the valley and check on her mother. I was surrounded by Jessica's images. My studio was covered in them. Drawings, etchings, linocuts, watercolours, oil studies, gouaches, those little black and white snapshots she gave me. A picture of her grandmother and herself standing by the gate to the garden ready to catch the school bus to Braidwood, the post-and-rail fence upright and straight. She's a schoolgirl. She's wearing a pleated tunic over a white blouse with short sleeves and she's not exactly smiling. There's something wistful and beautiful about her in this one. She's got her hair in plaits. Vulnerability, that's what it is, to time. The quick leap of time. It gives me a tight feeling in my stomach to look into this little picture of her. You can already see the build-up of her decision to leave her mother's garden and Lower Araluen. Her expectation of life. The uncertain outline of plans gathering in her expression. Her teachers telling her she's got a bright future. Otherwise she's the fourth Keal woman and is stuck in the valley forever. I can just make out the bed on the verandah behind them. I know her father's lying on the bed on the verandah outside the kitchen. There's just this one glimpse of her father. A blurry pale splodge. It's the only image she gave me of him. He's lying on this canvas bed and is facing up the hill towards the road and the walnut tree, as if that's where he's hoping to go when he recovers, not when he dies. Only he's not going to recover. His upper body is propped nearly to the vertical by a pile of pillows and rolled blankets. He looks as if he's about to launch himself in a last desperate leap. His face is all hollows and shadows. His cheeks are sucked in, his eyes are sunk far back in his head, there are dark cups at his temples, and a thin last wispiness of hair is on the point of becoming detached from his scalp. He's grey and unshaven and he's struggling to breathe. I'm remembering all this from what she's told me. Though it's surprising how much of this detail you can actually see in the photograph when you know what you're looking for. Beside him on the sill of the window there's a radio. A midweek race meeting is being called. Jessica was twelve when he died. He was in the bed on the verandah for years. She can't remember him any other way. He was an English seaman who jumped ship in Newcastle and made his way to the valley with the idea of working on the gold dredges. 'We lost contact with all our relatives,' she tells me. 'Mum and I are the last. There were no boys. Or there was one. No one knows where he got to. The men were temporary at the Keal place.' She says this with a laugh. 'In the beginning the men went after the gold, then they worked for the dredging companies, then they got jobs on the shire. They never did anything in the garden. Eventually they always left. Or maybe Gran kicked them out. She was never married to my moth- er's father. They weren't missed. My father was the only one who stayed. He had to take to his bed to do it. That's all I remember about him, the sound of the races on the radio or the cricket and him wheez- ing and struggling and staring at me as I go past.'

I'm doing the door-sized oil. The vertical portrait. This is it. This is the portrait. It's a picture of a woman sitting on a bed looking out of a window. It's her. It's her picture of herself. She rang me late at night, when it was lunchtime in London. She made the call from her bed in the hospital. We didn't talk for long. I was in bed when the phone went. I stayed in bed imagining her at the other end in her bed. 'What's that noise?' I asked her. 'I'll shut the door,' she said. 'Hang on a sec. It's people in the corridor.' Then her voice was quieter. As if we were in the same room. There's still a girl in her. I listen to her voice and I'd like to tell her certain things. Even now I'd like to explain that absence thing. To explain it fully. Even though she'd laugh and tell me not to be silly. She'd say, 'I know already, you don't have to explain anything to me.' I can hear her saying this. But I'd still like to. It would sound as though I was being self-absorbed. Which I am being. There's nothing to say.

'So when are you getting out?' I ask her. And she tells me she'll be out soon but doesn't have a date for it yet. But I don't believe her. Then she says Caroline's just arrived. Then we've hung up and we haven't said anything. I'm sitting up in bed on my own staring at *Henry* sliding sideways out of his own portrait.

I'm in the middle of the portrait when my son arrives without warning. This is the first time he's ever come on his own. 'Where's Sandy?' I ask him. 'Where are the kids?' But he doesn't want to talk about it.

'Have you got any beer, Dad?'

I point him at the fridge. What's going on? I put my hand on his arm and he stiffens and eases himself away from me. We used to have a cuddle. He gives me a sideways smile which I understand to mean he doesn't intend to try explaining anything to me because he thinks I wouldn't understand. I'm edgy. I need to get back to her portrait. It's waiting for me. He comes into the studio and looks at what I'm doing and we drink beer.

'What are you working on, Dad? Who's she? Do I know her?'

I realise I'm waiting for him to leave. There's nothing I can do for him. He's thirty-four. But he stays.

'I'll be right,' he says. 'You don't need to worry about me. Just get on with your work as if I'm not here.'

He's kidding, of course. He wanders out to the kitchen. But I can still see him from the studio. He's standing at the sink looking out the window. I can't work. He's being careful. He's keeping quiet so he won't disturb me. But it's not his noise that's disturbing me. I'd rather he started yelling and screaming and carrying on and told me what's bothering him than this creeping around. If it's none of my business, why has he come here? It's his home. It's where he grew up. He's left something here that bothers him. He doesn't know what it is. He doesn't know how to locate it.

He stays for a week. He hasn't brought anything with him. He doesn't go out. I go out. I bring the shopping back and I cook meals for both of us. He stands in doorways looking into rooms. I don't ask him to leave. I lie awake far into the night, thinking of her and listening to him. A door going. The flywire door creaking. What's he doing? He's sitting out the back with a beer. We don't talk.

I did some big charcoal drawings of her from life. These drawings are on heavy paper, they're four metres high by two metres wide. I used two step ladders. I did seven. They involved extreme foreshortening and narrow closeups. Three of them worked okay and I kept them. I destroyed the others. So I had this tryptich, like Japanese banners on the wall, as if I lived in a castle. Some people spend an entire year doing a town in central Victoria, or in Spain or France. I spend a year doing a woman or a man, or a family, a group. What's the difference? Is there more to a town than there is to a person? Flaubert said, *If I go so slowly, it's because a book for me is a special way of living.* Well that's a portrait for me. A way of living. My life, not someone else's. There's a whole show in it. Maybe two.

My son was standing up close to these big drawings staring at them. They are nude studies. Glimpses. Diagonals. Verticals. You don't see much. Mark, that's my son, is standing up close to these drawings of Jessica and he's staring at them for a long time. 'What do you think of them?' I asked him.

'How can you find these people interesting.'

There was a certain amount of contempt in the way he said this, as if he wished to imply that my entire life was some kind of a sham. 'Well,' I said. 'You know, they pay me. The money's very good.' I did that to confirm him. To let him think he was right about me.

'You never painted us. You never found us that interesting. Me and Mum.'

It's true of course and it hurts to hear him say it. He's talking about my weakness. But you reach a point where you cease trying to justify yourself. The first thing some people do then is to judge you harshly. And it turns out that's just what they've been waiting for an opportunity to do. For years. If you won't defend yourself then you must be a bastard and there's an end of it. He left in the morning. He'd made his point. It worried me of course. But there's only so much energy left. Either you use your energy for your work or you use it for something else.

His contempt for Jessica, for my project, for me, increased my energy for her. His contempt gave me more energy for my work. But it also got me gnawing away at the family connection while I was working with her material. There was this confusion of subject matter leaching into my work. It puzzled me. It excited me. I didn't know what I was really up to. I felt I was on the edge of finding something. I didn't dare to examine it.

I remember the hour he was born. I remember his first breath. The way his little blue body turned pink and he started to live for himself. I've forgotten a lot of other things, but I still remember that. 'Breathe!' I implored him. It was the moment I became vulnerable.

She sits on her old bed with her chin in her hand gazing out at her mother at work in the garden, and she wonders why she's come back. Her departure from the valley as a girl of eighteen was not blessed, but entailed the complexities and uncertainties of a renunciation, the ambivalence and the betrayals of abandoning her rights and titles, and her responsibilities; all those things for which she was held to be accountable by her mother and her grandmother; her *place*, in other words, the Keal place, the garden that her great-grandmother, Amelia Keal, had established in 1854, the year *her* husband came upon the first grains of gold ever to be seen by a European in the Araluen creek.

But the garden of the Keal women outlasted the men and the dredges and the gold. It outlasted the noise and the industry and the excitement and the tragedies and the disappointments and the heroes and the myths. Eccentric, determined and persistent, it outlasted them all. Lost to history. Jessica was a Keal woman. The fourth. She had gathered her courage and her dreams and had reversed Amelia's founding act. *She* had determined it must all come to an end, the eccentric persistence to no avail.

She brought with her these family likenesses and certain forgotten episodes of my childhood. Which is not something I'm prepared to try to explain. You could easily have three volumes of memoirs on that subject alone. All I know is nowadays I'm painting a portrait of my sister. That's what I'm up to. And there's plenty more to do. I'm even playing around with my father's portrait. I've done a few sketches. At the moment he looks like one of Dürer's old men. Jessica's mother. But maybe I'll improve on that. He's in the mirror whenever I want to have a look. I see him looking back at me. He's forgiven me, I think. I've got energy. I'm painting the absence and the silence of my childhood. These days I'm doing family portraits. There's not much information. No beautifully structured lives. Scraps and hints and glimpses and bits of old snapshots and a few memories. That's it. I can't ask them to sit for me. That's all there ever is. Fragments.

Some time after Jessica's mother died Caroline wrote to me about disposing of the place and I went down to have a last look. The agent was with a young couple in the kitchen. No smoking redgum log, however. The place was cold and filled with the smell of her mother's earth. They were tourists from Canberra looking for a hobby farm. So I bought the place before they could say a word. I paid twice what it was worth to them. I thought that was it. I intended to just let the old place rot away and fall into a heap. But I couldn't leave it alone. So here I am. I've been here ever since. I moved in. I shan't be moving out again. Michael approves. He thinks it's good for a successful artist to live in a place like this. 'An authentic Australian setting,' he calls it. 'This place has got distinction,' he says. He enjoys coming here. It makes a change from Sydney. He likes the broken post-and-rail fence. He's got plans. A larger studio, a bunkhouse for the guests. And so on. He likes bringing the buyers here. The admirers. The aficionados. He shows them around and takes them down to her bathing hole for a swim. This gives him a chance to strip off and flash himself. He's delighted about being a repulsive old man. I told him something about the walnut tree. We were sitting up there on the hill watching the evening and drinking some wine and not saying much.

'In a hard time,' I told him, 'this tree releases a poison from its roots. The poison kills its offspring and ensures its own survival.' Which was something she told me. He liked that. It appealed to him. Michael's the only one left who's known me all these years. We don't have to say anything. Even more than making money, which is really his mask, Michael cares for painters and painting. More than anyone else I've known. He doesn't want to own anything. Caring for painters is really his vocation. In the early days I didn't understand him. But maybe he didn't understand himself then either. He never met her. He regrets that.

'How come I never met her?' he asks whenever a reference to her comes up in the conversation. He suspects me of having intentionally kept her out of his way.

She woke herself with a great shuddering snore, lying on her back on the iron bed as if she'd been felled by a blow, her mouth agape, her throat dry and roasting, one naked leg unslung loosely over the side of the bed. She couldn't move. She was crippled in mind and body. She lay there puzzling as to where she could be. The light had mellowed. The day had weakened and was sliding away towards the hills. Light was no longer roaring outside and bouncing back from the window but was seeping into the room at a low, sneaky angle. Sidling in and washing about the little room. Searching for something. Seductive fingers of light seeking out the form of the woman on the bed, modelling her. A soft golden glow accumulating about the flesh of her naked thigh, flattering and caressing.

Now that the day is withdrawing the room has ceased to resist and is warm, and she has become all softly crumpled shadows and a sense of disarray. Her face is turned away from the viewer. She might be the victim of a brutal murder. A crime of passion. A momentary rage. A bedroom portrait. One of Sickert's sinisterly anecdotal fables, *The Sunday Visitor*. A violent death. You can still smell her visitor in the stuffy air, and smell their passion.

The story is my secret.

Jessica lay still after the passing of the snore, her mind dragging upward through her dreams, carrying to a distant surface she might never reach. That she might wish never to reach. A low, intermittent murmuring floating in the air. With an enormous effort she sat up. She groaned and pressed her hand to her chest. There was a hard lump of pain deep within her sternum. The disembodied murmur resolving into the sound of a motor vehicle. She breathes and massages the pain, remembering.

I destroyed several of these but three versions have survived. This last one, the one in which she's sitting up with her hand pressed to her chest and the room is almost in darkness, is once again a narrow, vertical painting, tightly enclosing the scene. Her pale arm and her pale thigh. Viewed at a diagonal through an exceedingly tall doorway. A big painting. One of my biggest. But just a glimpse of something, a concentration on this little moment that is driven inward by the tight framing of the doorway. It measures four metres high by one and half metres wide.

There's only one road through the Araluen Valley. The surface of this road is gravel. It scrambles past the Keal place a hundred metres or so up the hill, cutting an uneven path through the stringybark forest just beyond the walnut tree, which is not on Keal land but is on Forestry Commission land. Jessica sits on her bed massaging her chest and listening to the sound of the vehicle as it comes and goes, hollowing a space into the silence of the afternoon, then withdrawing out of earshot into a timbered gully, before returning again, louder than before, the illusion that it is getting closer, as if the driver has changed his mind and is coming back.

PENGUIN – THE BEST AUSTRALIAN READING

BOOKS BY ALEX MILLER IN PENGUIN

The Ancestor Game

Piecing together the puzzle of exiled artist Lang Tzu, last of a wealthy Chinese lineage, writer Steven Muir finds himself caught in a strange and haunted landscape. Both men know the solitude of the only child, and the exquisite poignancy of the relationship with parents. But beneath the familiar are the twisted threads of Lang's past – the sweep of ancestry and its lingering inheritance.

BOOKS BY ALEX MILLER IN PENGUIN

The Tivington Nott

To sacrifice or be sacrificed: the outsider's stark choice in Alex Miller's darkly violent Exmoor. But, like the almost mythical Tivington nott, the outsider harbours a savage will of his own, an Odyssean instinct for self-preservation the natives cannot tame. What they plan as a bloody initiation becomes for him a liberatory rite of passage.